JOHN DESTINY

John's Awakening

Andrew Carter

Gotham Books

30 N Gould St.
Ste. 20820, Sheridan, WY 82801
https://gothambooksinc.com/

Phone: 1 (307) 464-7800

© 2024 *Andrew Carter*. All rights reserved.

No part of this book may be reproduced, stored in a retrieval system, or transmitted by any means without the written permission of the author.

Published by Gotham Books (April 5, 2024)

ISBN: 979-8-88775-853-4 (P)
ISBN: 979-8-88775-854-1 (E)

Because of the dynamic nature of the Internet, any web addresses or links contained in this book may have changed since publication and may no longer be valid.

The views expressed in this work are solely those of the author and do not necessarily reflect the views of the publisher, and the publisher hereby disclaims any responsibility for them.

TABLE OF CONTENTS

Foreword By Sue Trudgian v

Introduction By Andrew Carter vii

The Third Floor 1

    Day One 4

    Two Weeks Later: 43

    Two Weeks Later: 94

About the Author 139

    Forthcoming Books of the Series: 140

Foreword

By Sue Trudgian

When Andrew asked me to write a piece about how I felt when typing this book, I was delighted! It never felt like work because I quickly got caught up with the characters and their stories. I grew to know them and I formed judgements about them. I was soon to learn that those judgements came from my first floor consciousness and that they would change over the pages as I got to know the characters better. You'll find out what I mean.

I was always eager to get the next set of manuscript pages for typing because I wanted to know where Andrew was taking his characters - or maybe that should read 'where the characters were taking Andrew'! One thing I found though, John is *exhausting* to follow around! He seems to jump from one situation to another, sometimes without drawing breath!

These books about John's life are funny in parts and I often found myself laughing out loud at his antics. They are also very moving as Andrew has a good grasp on human emotion and there is real learning to be had from John's escapades and the different ways he deals with life as he moves to higher levels of consciousness. I have actually found myself in real life situations where I wondered what level of consciousness my reactions had come from. If the first floor consciousness, I pondered what I would have done differently had I been reacting from a second or third floor consciousness.

As someone who enjoys reading, for me a book should leave me satisfied, yet wanting more; be mysterious, but realistic; it should stir up a wide spectrum of emotions; allow me to form a connection with its characters; and if I learn something, then that's a big bonus. It has fulfilled that criteria and I am certainly left wanting more!

I invite you to step into John's world and *allow yourself to be changed.*

Introduction

By Andrew Carter

This book was a complete surprise to me. I had the idea of its title and what it related to in regards to presenting three levels of consciousness, which is the way the book starts. It then, completely out of the blue, turned itself into a story. I hesitated whether to take it in that direction, but I have learnt to write what comes into my head without questioning it or logically trying to plan it out.

You will see where the story starts - it opens "The alarm bell rings", and it revolves around the events and circumstances that create John's awakening. John is not a mythical character, as you will see. He gets himself into some real predicaments, which is all part of his journey, which prizes him out of his first floor consciousness.

Many of you will relate to John on one level or another, or maybe even Helen, Trevor, Linda, Janet or Miranda. John's journey is full of humour, joy, sadness and romance. I found myself laughing whilst writing and also crying. The book gives a very powerful message as it portrays real-life situations and how a mysterious silence surrounds John at key moments of decision.

The book revolves around three days in the life of John, each of these days are two weeks apart. If the obstacles that are presented to John from Day One are overcome, then they are not repeated. If not, they present themselves to John slightly differently, but they carry the same message to him.

The mysterious silence John comes to recognise, and he starts to be able to create it himself in times of need. This silence, the book reveals, is the energy of the second floor consciousness, and it starts to change the way John feels, thinks and acts.

The significant part of this change is when he meets Miranda and this acts as a catalyst for his awakening, because as the book states, "John has something to do in this life." We can all relate to that statement as we all possess potential destiny.

This book is very different from many spiritual books, as it enables the Reader to find the key messages through John's encounters for their own awakening, and the main thing is that through those encounters, it enables you to think about them because of the insights John receives.

The humour at times can, to someone who is very serious about their spiritual enlightenment, seem to be of no spiritual value, but the message is that humour is a way of overcoming life's difficulties, therefore humour and joy lead you into the second floor consciousness.

I hope you enjoy reading this book. I am sure John would agree with that.

The Third Floor

Three floors, three aspects, three places of living experience, can you conceive that you exist upon three floors simultaneously? Are you the same person living these three simultaneous existences, from the viewpoint of the person residing upon the second floor, to the person that now maybe is reading these words? The answer could be quite different from what you think it would be. Look out now wherever you are, into the area and space within which you are at this moment in time and realise everything within it belongs to the first floor, and the first floor is at ground level. Look out of the window and observe what your vision sees, the buildings, the people, everyone fulfilling a role, they may be going shopping, going to work, all the many things that cause the person to be moving within the space fulfilling, or attempting to fulfil, a task. Realise the pain and pleasure of this physical experience, realise how we have developed over the centuries and the technology that now exists today. The first floor is physical, but it is also a reflection of the second floor in many ways.

Let us consider the human being as he moves within the space and what he has created to increase that speed of movement. In a sense, humanity has sped things up. Imagine the rapid movement of energy, for example upon a motorway, and then think about the plants, the trees, the grass, their movement is towards the Sun, and they are firmly rooted into the Earth, but the soil provides their nourishment and the light provides their growth. The crystals and minerals are the structure of the planet, they are the foundation of the first floor, then there are the animals and birds. So the first floor consists of four kingdoms each one feeding the other.

What is the purpose of all this, is it just the way it is? Or is there a higher intelligence, a creator? Are all these kingdoms, and the many species existing within them, totally separate? They all fall within a category, for example the birds, they all fly as such but there are many species. Are all these separate from one another? Is a human being a separate entity from another human being and their only unity is the fact that, collectively, they are called humanity?

So all that exists upon the Earth has happened as part of evolution, the ability to evolve, to change and adapt to environment and circumstances, but what allows for that to happen?

Why does the Earth itself continue to change?

Is all life a part of the same thing, or is it separate?

It is impossible for it to be separate, and yet the first floor is a place of separation. Many people believe their separation is quite normal and they are above the laws of nature. This is not a conscious thing it is just the way it has evolved.

The first floor, you could say, is like a schoolroom, and the lessons concern light, love and life. This is just an analogy, it is nothing like a schoolroom as you understand it from your own experience of "growing up." That is an interesting statement and of course this concerns development, mainly upon the first floor, but where does all that lead? Well, we shall see. Let us follow John to work.

DAY ONE

The alarm clock shrills its message into the space, the room resounds to its repetitive sound growing louder by the second, a hand reaches out and misses the clock knocking it over, grunt-like sounds were heard, as John rolled out of bed in pursuit of the alarm clock he had knocked across the wooden floor. The sound abruptly came to an end. John had made it out of bed, the covers of his bed in a dishevelled heap; John paused trying to achieve some sort of brain consciousness.

"Ha," he thought, "It's Friday!" But before he could become too happy about this prospect another thought came to him, it dawned on him that it was actually Wednesday – more grunts followed that seemed to form some kind of sequence, which obviously came from the "not wanting to go to work" English Dictionary. Having recovered his poise, accepting his fate, he rushed downstairs hoping to recover lost time. John had a habit of cutting things fine. He hadn't quite worked it out yet that one had to allow for unforeseen circumstances, and today he hadn't.

The shirt he was going to iron the night before lay on the floor in a crinkled mess. More words from the alternative dictionary were spoken, which continued to weave themselves into some sort of thrash metal vocals when he realised his last pair of socks had entered the washing basket the night before but, no surprise, there was no space available, so they laid upon the floor looking at him, inviting him to test them out. It had been quite a warm day yesterday, and John was a little prone to requiring more than one pair of socks in a day. But things were a little desperate, without thinking he grabbed them, putting them to his nose. John was a little slow in retrieving his senses first thing and things were slow to register, a brief moment of silence before he activated his sense of smell. What follows can only be described as a higher tonal rendition of his previous creative endeavour, but this time he had shifted his polarity into Hip Hop, his movements were quite stunning as he projected the socks into space. John has a flair for creative word expression. There was only one thing for it, he decides, as he launches his head into the washing basket seeking the least smelly pair of socks. Finally, he pulled a pair out. (I think by now his sense of smell had retreated, as the early morning onslaught was far too much for it!)

Arm stretched out and with the socks dangling from between his fingers, decision made, this was the least smelly pair he can find, or were they? Unfortunately, this particular pair had already suffered misuse and there, staring John in the face, was a hole. There was a moment of silence, as his brain descends into his stomach; it tightened, unable to cope with John's sonic thought, instant mental indigestion as his trousers tightened, his stomach became bloated with mental thoughts. "Ha," but John possessed a wonderful self-defence mechanism developed from early childhood, where he could overcome disappointment by making some sort of joke of it all. He worked it out in an instant that the hole in the sock was nothing worse than a hole in his underpants, because both were covered up, the former with his shoes and the latter with his trousers.

Suddenly, his brain consciousness sparked into reality, "What was the time?" Time was unforgiving, in that it does not stop while there is a crisis concerning the day's attire, as this is the first floor, and that is one thing that cannot be brought to a standstill, John needed to work with time, not against it. Time had been swallowed up in his socks and shirt. He charged downstairs, almost out of the door he stopped, as if he had hit an invisible barrier. "Lunch," he thought throwing open the fridge door. John was confronted with his duality, the fridge was not exactly brimming with a variety of food. He stared into the fridge.

Now, if you can imagine his mental thoughts, there would be two Johns standing there, one that was definitely going to take to work the salad box and the yoghurt pot. Now, this particular self was quite new into John's consciousness, it had only come into existence through the moaning of his mother, who had been a dominant figure in his life to improve his diet.

For a brief moment his hand was reaching for the salad, an amazing thing then occurred, the second John took control, and his hand instantly went to the second shelf in an almost poetic movement, securely placing his hand on the steak and kidney pie that he had previously attempted to hide whilst he was being his other self. The fridge door closed then some sort of instinctual reaction happened, the bar of chocolate, the bag of crisps and the bottle of Coke flashed rapidly into his lunch-box and with no remorse, he now was his dominant self.

He left and jumped into his car about to go careering off the drive – well, that would have been the case but something else happened, he had thrown his engine into rapid life, revved it up, rammed it into gear and was about to let the handbrake off – it was at this moment something stopped him. He couldn't explain what, but some sort of silence came over him, then a thought came into his head. "You need to calm down, you might have an accident and run into something, it is not worth it." He slowed his engine down and pulled slowly off the drive but not quite, he had to let the mother and baby in the pram go past first. He drove down the road thinking how strange that all was, the more he thought about it, the more he started to wonder whether it was some sort of premonition. He had read about those sorts of things, thinking "What a load of old rubbish." So he rationalised it all out as being a coincidence.

But *what* caused him to stop? What created that brief moment of silence, and what impressed his consciousness with the thought that slowed him down? There are no coincidences, this was a small tap from the second floor.

John's journey to work was about 20 minutes, he took the same route every day; John gained his security through repetition. That brief moment of silence was now gone. He watched the clock willing it not to move, as he encountered one obstacle after the other, first in the form of a bus and then the most awful thing someone can encounter if they were late a, *Learner Driver*! Almost instantly he found himself reciting words from his alternative dictionary, this time there were sporadic pauses, almost as if he was collecting the appropriate words. Another brief moment as John told himself that he was a learner driver once, instantly followed by "not as #@**@! bad as that!."

Now, John was also trying to cut down his smoking, another thing his mother had pointed out to him, this all had happened on his last visit, he had almost been summoned to go and see her. He had tried to get out of it, unfortunately he had run out of excuses, and John was very good at excuses, (but not as good as his mother, she knew them all!) John was very predictable. He did worry at the time, when his mother invited him in, she made him feel comfortable, got him a drink and, he had noticed, she had locked the door and taken the key out. He had been set up for a fatal character assassination, the opening line was, "John, I would like to have a little word with you." It depends how you view what was meant by a "little word" – it certainly wasn't. Two hours later, John crawled out of his mother's house thinking, "she always does something like this, as if I am not depressed enough." The car, on automatic pilot, took him to the pub. That was two days ago, and John was still reeling from that event, let alone the effects of the alcohol he had consumed over the past two nights.

The learner driver he had encountered that morning on the way to work, obviously picked up on John's energies, as the car started acting like a kangaroo. John managed to prise a cigarette out of its packet in sheer desperation with his teeth. "Now where's that ?@@**@! lighter?" Wedging his hand into his pocket, the seat belt not helping, out came a lighter. A fleeting panicky thought, "Will it work?" It did, and John lit his cigarette just in time before he had a nervous breakdown. This three inch stick of tobacco instantly brings in some sort of control. A funny thing happened once he stopped directing abuse at the learner driver, as if by magic the car turned off leaving John with a clear road.

"Thank God for that," he thought, only half a mile to go. Some sort of smile came over his face, as he drew his last puff of the cigarette, and threw it towards the side window. The smile instantly disappeared as he saw the lighted cigarette bounce off the unopened window, it was then as if time stood still, the cigarette slowly passed by his vision on its descent, time then instantly sped up again and the smell of burning reached his nostrils, "Oh shit it has fallen between my legs!" Looking to pull the car over in panic, John went into jockey mode, the steering wheel became the reins of a horse, up and down he went, until he screeched to a halt at the side of the road and leapt out of the car with unbelievable speed, with which he was not normally accustomed.

The cigarette was smouldering on his seat. He takes action and launches the cigarette out of the car into the road. Now, it was a good job a cyclist was not passing, but John had a reputation for instant re-actions.

A small hole stared at him from his seat, not only that but he had a small hole in his trousers, your imagination will know where it was. Panic over, he resumed his driving position and shut the car door. About to start the car, something strange happened again, there was a moment of silence and what came into his head was quite a revelation for John. He realised that if he had not been so frustrated at the learner driver, then that might not have happened. In fact, he starts to think about other incidents that were related to his frustration, where there were similar repercussions. But while he was in this state of thinking his eyes fell upon the clock, his moment of deep thought swiftly ended as his first floor consciousness equates the time to the time he was supposed to be at work.

Amazingly enough, John makes it to work with a minute to spare. In he strode heading for his desk. Now John was normally quite oblivious to atmospheres as he was, technically speaking, always within his own atmosphere. He wondered why he was sensing an unsettled atmosphere.

"This is strange," he thought to himself, "there is nobody new here, and everyone looks the same."

Now John was not to know that Jane was worried about her father, and Justin had been involved in a blazing row with his wife before he left this morning. Nobody was talking about these things, but a slight change had occurred in John, of which he was not aware, but he was aware that things didn't feel right.

He shrugged it all off and sat down at his desk, not exactly prepared for the day. There were numerous calls to make, but the first call came to him, a customer enquiring about a certain stock item. Now this was a multi-buy, and John's brain automatically calculated what it was worth, and the fact that it would boost his sales figures to make a pretty good month, he had also calculated how much money would be made, all this whilst talking to the customer. He also knew that a competitor was offering the item far cheaper. John had the ability to discount, but he would lose some of his bonus. John was very good at selling and saw it as a challenge. He had a first floor consciousness that saw competition as a way of making money.

John went through his usual flamboyant selling act, it was most convincing and just as he was about to clinch the deal, at the best price for John, the customer told John that he trusted him to give him the best price he could offer. John's thought patterns stumbled, he apologised to the customer and told him that his computer was messing him about, but another moment of silence had entered and this had totally thrown John. He started to feel he was not telling the truth and could do better. His alter ego dismisses this, but it wouldn't go away. John's duality was fighting between the true and the false. To John's dismay his ego relinquished control and he told the customer that he could offer him a 20% discount on the goods, this had just popped up on his screen. The deal was concluded, John's bonus or the majority of it had disappeared down the toilet and this "other self" had pulled the chain! A period of no thinking then occurs, until to John's dismay, his ego self came battering back in to take control. John then proceeded to acclaim how stupid he had been and wondered what came over him. John soon adjusts to the situation in true fashion and proceeds upon a selling blitz.

Lunchtime was approaching and John remembered that there was a lunchtime relaxation class, organised by the company to try to reduce the stress and sick leave. John had forgotten and was totally unprepared. Lunchtime came and the office filed into the meeting for their stress-reducing session.

John had no preconceived thoughts upon this, just the fact that he didn't want to be there. His negativity concerning this could be perceived at a great distance. But he had no choice as the office was being overshadowed by Trevor the assistant manager.

Everyone was greeted by Miranda, a specialist in relaxation, Yoga and meditation. She had laid out the room beautifully with yoga mats, incense was burning and melodic music was playing. To John, stepping into this room was not what he wanted to do. "Welcome John," Miranda said. "Just take off your shoes and find a place upon the mat." That sentence instantly triggered his memory impulses, he couldn't move and he couldn't speak, all he could think about was his socks. Basically his shoes were like the dam holding back the water, but in this case the "smell," not only that, there was a hole. He couldn't go back and he couldn't go forward, but then, Miranda almost pushed him into the room, and at that same point the answer came, take the socks off! In an instant he spotted a bag in the corner, and with sheer grace of movement, removed his shoes and socks and deposited them into the empty plastic bag, then he took his place on the mat.

Relaxing, he tentatively sniffed the space around him, trying to detect any sign of his smelly feet. Just a faint detection, but then you would have to be very close for anyone to notice.

John felt safe and secure at last and started to relax, he even managed a smile. He wouldn't have, if he'd known at that moment, the bag wasn't exactly empty! It contained some CDs that Miranda had brought for the session. Just then the music finished, it was the welcoming pre-session CD. Miranda walked across the room to her bag for the opening session CD. John followed her movements, at first unaware as to where she was going, consequently he was still in a smiling state of satisfaction thinking he had solved his problems of potential self-embarrassment. Now some people would take all this in a light-hearted manner, but obviously due to the situation probably not many. Saving face was a big issue, especially for John, as his father, along with his mother (although very different in their approach), were very authoritarian with fixed opinions and views, and in a way, slightly lacking any sense of humour. In fact, the family dog had more humour, and all it could do was bark.

So let us pause and imagine John's face, as Miranda's hand reached in to her bag for a CD. Now if John was a child he probably would have done a runner at this point, and this was exactly what he did - with the excuse of the toilet. But before he can reach the door he heard a voice

"Hey John," it was Miranda, "do you want your socks?" He turned to see Miranda in exactly the same position as he had been first thing this morning, arm outstretched with this socks dangling from her fingertips. John paused, then walked over and took the socks, thanking her, she whispered to him, "I saw you put them in my bag, don't worry about it, I had the same problem this morning." She gave him a hug and said "see you in a minute."

Touched by her compassion, John felt very moved, in fact all his stress disappeared and a small tear formed at the corner of his eye. He went to the toilet, as a matter of course due to the situation, and stood looking at himself in the mirror. His ego first floor nature had gone and he started to see another John. The silence was heard once more and John became caught in time, his mental overdrive had come to a stop as he became transfixed at what he saw in the mirror. He had never really looked at himself in this way, there had never been time. Perhaps John's heart centre was beginning to open.

His day so far suddenly flashed though his mind, this was the third time this had happened today, but this encounter with Miranda was different, she had been nice to him and gave him a hug. Could this mean she actually cared? John thought. He couldn't analyse this, it was all too other than his experience, so for once, he didn't.

He went back to the class and took his place on the mat, Miranda had waited for his return. She gave a short talk about stress and then proceeded with relaxation and meditation techniques. In half an hour it was over and the next session would be in two weeks' time. John thanked Miranda, and then totally out of character, started to tell her some of his problems. Just at the point, when he was really starting to open up, he cut it short and said "Goodbye," and walked away.

"John" Miranda says.

John stopped and looked back, "Yes?"

"I understand you know."

He paused, then said, "Thank you, Miranda," and walked back to his desk. Before he could really pull his chair up the phone rang, this was John's biggest customer. During the conversation John sensed that he was going to make a big buy. Then, to his surprise his customer started to say that he had been on the brink of changing his supplier, but had a conversation with John's previous customer. (Remember the one that John had given the 20% discount to? Yes, that one where he thought how ""?@@**@! stupid he had been, but that act of stupidity had saved John from losing his biggest customer.) John clinched a very big deal with his biggest customer, it was fair and John gave as much discount as he was allowed to, but because of the size of the order it boosted his monthly sales bonus way above his previous record. John was now starting to realise the meaning of truth, although not consciously aware of this.

He put the phone down, a small smile came over his face, "What a day this had been," he thought. Then he started to think about things, he started to reflect… if he hadn't discounted the order in the morning, he would have lost his biggest customer. So he surmised that he was not so stupid after all. He also reflected that all this had occurred after one of those points of silence. Maybe, he thought, those moments affected him in a positive way, allowing him to make the right decisions and actions. "But why were they happening and where did they come from?" He thought.

John was starting to respond to the "second floor," John had lived his life upon the "first floor," now it seems the door to the second floor was starting to open, but John as yet, couldn't perceive or register the door, as he hadn't climbed the stairs – but he had taken the first step as he was starting to think about relationships. In this instance, how positive action based upon truth created more positive action. Regarding this morning's discount, that was positive action based on truth outward from John, and in the second case from his biggest customer, it was positive reciprocal action inwards. In short, in the first instance John was radiatory of truth, and in the second he was magnetic through this to the positive energy attracted to him. John was now thinking about Cause and Effect which he will come to realise as he starts to climb the stairs, and this will be in consciousness. Unless of course he chooses not to, but then John had something important to do in this life. It was his destiny.

John was still reflecting and was on the brink of certain discoveries when he was jolted abruptly out of his inner thoughts. Helen, the office manager, stood in front of John, as John was deep in thought he didn't see her coming, therefore he was unprepared for her presence. Normally

John's technique for manager survival was to register immediately her approach, he scans her demeanour to then adopt the necessary defence mechanism. Too late, there she stood. She then proceeded to pull up a seat and started to inform John that the company was not too happy with his performance, and that his figures over the last three months had been down. John thought, it can't be that serious otherwise he would be in her office, which was exactly what she told him, but not quite.

"I was considering letting you go John, as things are a little tight at the moment." She had that stone-faced look and that normally means someone was out.

Helen had adapted to the role of manager very well as she had managed years ago, to completely negate any emotional feelings. However, she did at times suffer indigestion problems, which she attributed to certain foods not agreeing with her, nothing to do with her emotions of course? She also suffered on and off with a lower back problem, obviously nothing to do with the problems she had with her husband due to her lack of emotions and sensitivity? But she did find it quite strange that every time they had a row her back played up…? Helen had learned to block her emotions, as she felt they would be in the way if she was going to be successful.

A silence followed, not the silence John had encountered a few times earlier, this was more of a silent panic. Waiting for her next word, his auric field had withdrawn inward and created a barrier in case he heard the words that he didn't want to hear.

Helen went on to say, "How can I let you go after the large order you have secured today? Well done." and she walks away. John slumped over his desk thinking, "That was tricky. Oh well, best try to build upon my success." He was about to pick up the phone when Miranda came into his mind with the words, "Don't worry John I understand." Nobody had ever said that to him, and in that moment part of John's defence mechanism fell away, although he was not aware of it, not yet. He found himself thinking about Miranda, well she was quite attractive. Once more he was abruptly knocked out of his thought pattern.

"Hey, fancy having a coffee John?" It was Linda. John tried to avoid Linda as he had inadvertently promised to buy her a drink after work one night, it was in a moment of weakness, as far as he was concerned, after she had pestered him. This was his opinion, and just as he thought about it Linda followed with "And what about that drink you promised me, how about tonight?" It was as if Linda had read John's mind, thoughts are very powerful things.

John had exhausted his excuses, and not wishing to lose face, agreed. He also agreed to the coffee as he needed a fix of caffeine.

"See you later," Linda says. John slumped back onto his desk. "Why did I agree to that?" he thought, "She reminds me of my mother! On top of that I think she fancies me."

The afternoon was pretty mundane compared to the rest of the day and John managed to set up a couple of meetings. Things business-wise were still going well, but what about his personal life, or we could say his personality life?

He had certainly had some realisations, but would he allow his personality to gain from these experiences and thereby become nourished by them? Or just return to his normal personality self, based upon past experiences reflected in present circumstances? John's personality was somewhat surprised. He didn't know how to have fun, or experience the joy of life, and time and time again things had happened that reflected how John thought and felt, but as yet he hadn't related to it. He just saw life as it was, with no correspondences or connectivity. He basically went from one disaster to another and, of course, sometimes sank into self-pity and depression, and it was that depression that sent him to seek help. Consequently he was on anti-depressants, which kept things more level, but suppressed any remaining joy in life.

The end of the working day came and before he could pack his stuff away Linda was there.

"OK John, where are we going?" John really wanted to go home as he still had a problem with his socks, but as he was six feet tall there was a long way between his nose and his socks, therefore he could put them out of his mind.

"Where the hell am I going to take her?" he thought. "Somewhere busy would be a good solution." His mind instantly registered all the places within a five mile radius and he decided upon the Beeswing. "That is always busy" he thought. John hadn't been there for several years and he had forgotten why.... this was the place where his ex-wife frequented.

"Where are we going?" asks Linda. "OK, I will meet you there."

It would have been so easy just to drive home but, for some reason, he needed to go. They both pulled up into the car park, yes it looked busy, John pulled in first. He had decided recently that he ought to reverse into spaces, as he was prone to reversing out problems, but he couldn't be bothered tonight. Walking over to Linda he spotted a car that looked familiar, I think it was the weird thing hanging from the mirror which triggered his memory cells, but nothing came to mind. Being some sort of gentleman he opened the door for Linda and followed her in.

Here we leave John's journey for a while to shed some light upon his day so far. You will have gathered John needs to find himself, his true self. The second floor had impressed his consciousness several times and because of this, it had stopped John being reckless pulling away from his driveway. Another lesson came in the form of the learner driver. He also experienced himself being truthful, for which he wondered why he had been so stupid, but then look at what occurred as a result of this. But one thing that had a profound effect upon him were just those few words Miranda had spoken to him, "It's all right John, I understand." Isn't it true that sometimes all you need is for someone to understand you, no complications, no intrusive advice, but just a recognition. And sometimes advice can be very misleading as it tends to be based upon a person's own experience, and if this advice is based upon a purely first floor experience, then it will be separatist in nature and not help the person towards any sort of harmony or progression in life.

Now if advice came from a second floor consciousness, then it will be worth listening to, as already seen with John's experiences so far. Whereas if the advice, or in his mother's case some sort of command (based upon her own principles and morals; the problem here is that principles and morals tend to be very fixed and rigid). A "first" floor principle is very controlling and restricts freedom of choice. Give it a thought, how many principles of that nature may be governing your life? A second floor principle is something totally different, as it doesn't enforce rules because it doesn't have to, you either understand the second floor or you haven't arrived there yet.

One thing needs to be mentioned and that is that first floor principles hold the mind upon the first floor. Now a first floor mind will find that hard to believe, this is where the challenge lies and this is what John is now experiencing, but then experiences can start to speed up once a channel is starting to be created.

At the beginning it was said to look out at where you are and what you see. Now look out and listen to what you hear, is it based upon the first floor? Do not try to compare the second floor as this may mislead you. It was trying at first to see what many things are based upon. Ask yourself, are they based upon intelligence, love and purpose? If not then you will be starting to discriminate what is the will for good or what is the will for the self. Is what you hear based upon the higher concepts of life? Is what you hear emotional or self-created? To give you a clue to the second floor, this second floor consciousness will discriminate all these things and more, but will not criticise or judge, it will make observations. Hold this in your mind, because the first floor is separatist, so if you criticise or judge then you will be coming from the first floor consciousness which is based upon selfishness. Now to understand this, to embody the second floor concepts is not from a first floor experience, so you have to dissect the first floor experiences to arrive at the true reality of them. The first floor is the foundation of physical experience and has its natural laws, the second floor being new experiences. It is beyond the first floor, related to the physical, but in the analogy of a house; both are a part of the same building and the building rises upwards in a vertical ascent. If we relate this to consciousness, then to enter the second floor consciousness is to negate any of the first floor consciousness that will imprison you in the first floor, and that is exactly what it is, a prison for the Soul.

Everybody has a Soul, even upon the first floor, but if the mind is stuck upon the first floor then the Soul is imprisoned within it. Creativity is a second floor expression and what we call intuitive response, because think about this; the second floor receives the consciousness of three aspects, these being what we have previously mentioned, and these come from the third floor. Now once you have discriminated the first floor, and this takes a certain amount of thinking, but not ordinary thinking as one perceives that aspect, this is done in a relaxed alert manner without any stress or precondition, meaning you have to accept that your mind will be able to formulate the truth and go beyond your present experience. John is starting to receive the energy of the second floor, and this is now starting to change his perception, although there is a long way to go. John is destined to do this, it now remains as to whether he can start to integrate these experiences within his present consciousness. This could transform his life. Because life hasn't been easy, and it never is from a first floor consciousness, because he hasn't understood what has been happening. Now is his chance to open the door into the second floor consciousness, but to do this there are certain challenges, as we have previously mentioned and one of these is about to manifest in the form of, well let us continue his story then you can enter into his challenge, if there is a similarity of experience.

John and Linda have just entered the Beeswing. He looked for a space at the bar to order a drink, he actually quite needed this drink, understandable considering the day. There was a small gap at the bar.

"Can I have a small glass of white wine please John?" John leant at the bar, it was busy. Now John normally struggles to get served at the bar, it is almost as though he doesn't get noticed, which frustrates him a lot, another thing that can happen is the barrel runs out when he finally does get served. Obviously no connection with his frustration? But tonight he was starting to wonder if there was.

As he stood there waiting to be served an idea came to him, perhaps if he flashed and waved in the air a fifty-pound note he might get noticed, it worked and John ordered, the barrel didn't run out, and he paid. Feeling good about himself he picked the drinks up.

Now what happens when one is starting to perceive the second floor, a first floor challenge comes in to keep you there, and it did! He accidentally nudged the woman who stood with her back to him, she turned round, and there he was face to face with his ex-wife. Now if things had ended up harmonious this wouldn't have presented a problem. But they didn't, and the normal way of things is that she makes remarks based upon John's guilt, but also to get her own back, as she felt very resentful towards John. So there they are face to face. John instantly became an overheated stone statue, there was a glint in his ex-wife's eyes and then John made the fatal mistake, it just came out of his mouth.

"Hello, how are you?" Now normally the social response, even if that is not how you feel, would follow "I'm fine, I'm great, I'm good." John briefly realised what he has said and braced himself, but then suddenly a quiet silence came over him, which seemed to also descend on the pub as the level of noise started to subside.

Almost in slow motion her response came and true to form her opener was, "How do you think I am after you left me?" And then it continued, John normally tries to defend himself ending up with him losing his temper, but tonight that wasn't the case, his ex-wife paused to let John respond and of course whatever his response would be, would then inflame the situation.

He quietly looked her in the eyes and said, "I understand, take care of yourself," and walked away to the table to join Linda. That totally defused the situation and left his ex-wife speechless as she watched him sit down, she then turned away to continue the conversation she was having.

John had been told this earlier by Miranda and it had touched him, and now he had passed it on. John had showed love and compassion towards his ex-wife, even though she was blaming him for the break up. John sat down, placed the drinks on the table and started to think once more about that silence that had changed his response.

"Are you all right, John?" said Linda, who had looked a little uncomfortable. Linda didn't want to pry too much and mention his ex-wife, although she was not aware of who this other woman was. John commented he was fine and then wondered what else Linda was going to say, as in his first floor mind, John thought Linda had designs for him, in short fancied him and saw this as an opportunity to create a relationship, but John didn't particularly fancy her. He tended to go for physical appearance, how strange this is from a second floor mind, but to transcend the first floor takes many stages and realisations and in one day John hadn't arrived at that one.

But that wasn't Linda's intention at all. She started to explain to John that she thought he was lonely, very rarely smiled and needed a friend to help cheer him up. She thought he carried the weight of the world upon his shoulders and was possibly depressed. Apologising for her openness she continued.

"I only want to help because …." there was a slight pause, a moment of silence, "I understand." There it was again.

"She understands," he thought. This is all too much of a coincidence; although there are no coincidences, all things happen according to how things are. She proceeded to explain to John that he reminded her of herself some years ago and had recognised it in him.

"It happened some weeks ago," she said. "I was sitting at my desk looking over at you and suddenly everything went quiet and still. I then realised that I needed to help you. I am sorry for being so forward in getting you to buy me a drink. By the way, it took some weeks to get you out. I knew it would because I am not very attractive and need to lose some weight."

John had been so wrong about Linda, and he knew it now. What followed happened in his mind very quickly. It went from feeling very guilty, a reaction from his first floor mind, to then feeling that someone cared and of course understood him, again the first floor mind, could he trust her? Now trust is based upon discrimination and identification, from the second floor came the answer. "If she wants nothing from you and you want nothing from her, then you can trust". John thanked Linda and told her she was right.

"I am in not so good a place at the moment, and it would be nice to have a really good friend." How odd, John thought to have a friend that is a woman.

With all that out of the way John relaxed and started to talk openly with Linda. It was difficult, as every so often his defence mechanism reared up, but his experiences of the day had started to change his way of thinking and he instantly recognised it. Eventually the conversation went to that tricky subject of his socks, John was starting to see the funny side of it, especially concerning Miranda. Linda told John that she had helped organise the session as she went to a meditation class that Miranda ran.

"By the way John, that silence you mentioned sounds a bit like what can happen in meditation." Now John's impression of meditation was nothing like Linda's and he couldn't imagine himself sitting in a corner cross-legged with funny clothes on with incense burning and strange music.

"I'll tell you a little about the group John," said Linda. "There are all different types of guided meditations, we use crystals and sometimes healing. We get to learn about the human energetic system, even about sacred geometry. By the way, there is no music or incense and you sit in a chair."

"Well," thought John, it is almost as if she had read his mind. "What is this sacred geometry?" asked John as he was into numbers, but not quite in the same way as sacred geometry, well not at the moment. Linda did her best but she had limited knowledge.

"Miranda could tell you," said Linda, "why don't you come to the group?" John was not quite ready for that and said he would think about it. Linda announced that she had to leave soon.

"OK," said John, "thanks for the chat, perhaps we could do this again?"

"That would be great" said Linda. Now came the point of exit, only one slight problem, he had to walk past his ex-wife. He hadn't really taken any notice of her during his chat with Linda but now he did.

"Perhaps I can just move quickly past her without being noticed." It was all going well, his ex-wife was in deep conversation. Just as he thought he had got away with it, Linda stopped virtually right next to her.

"Hang on John I have left my keys on the table." She turned and went back, but also his ex-wife started to turn, he couldn't move, she looked straight at him, the person she was talking to also looked straight at him. "Here we go," John thought.

"You off then, John?"

"Yes."

"Take care then."

Linda had arrived back and they left. John's temperature returned to normal and he was slightly dumfounded with his ex-wife's response.

"See you at work tomorrow," Linda said with a smile, and gave John a quick hug. Linda jumped into her car and drove off.

John was in a slight trance, I think the day had caught up with him, slowly he got into his car and guess what? He entered into silence as he was trying to assimilate his experiences, but his mind had slowed down, he just sat there not thinking at all. Then certain thoughts came into his mind, he wasn't thinking and yet thoughts were entering. The thoughts were a bit of a mixture, but one thought pattern started to become dominant and that was his mother! Lots of situations concerning his mother flashed into his mind and he was suddenly starting to realise the massive influence she had had upon his life. "That's why I am not very confident sometimes," thought John. "She doesn't give me advice, she tells me what to do. She's always told me what to do. She constantly grinds me down. She tries to control me all the time." You can get the gist of what was going on in John's mind.

Then the big one hit him and that concerned his relationships, John thought really hard about this, reliving those interactions when his wife or partner was with him and his mother. She really hasn't done my relationships any good, she never liked any of them, they were never good enough. His ex-wife had tried to tell him, but John at that time couldn't acknowledge that, he just buried his head in the sand. But now he really saw it. "How could I have not seen this before?"

Well sometimes we don't, certain levels of our senses become numbed to external influences, therefore they don't register fully in the brain awareness. John had switched off certain levels of his senses, partly as a defence mechanism and a means of survival. There is another factor concerning this also, and that can be experienced upon an energetic level, his mother's energy. Meaning her interactions with John, and probably a lot of other people, were so strong that they had the power to diminish John's own power. He hadn't come to that conclusion yet, as John knows nothing of those things, well at least not yet. His final conclusion was that his relationship with his mother was one of the reasons for his unhappiness and, at times, depression. Now John nearly got onto the subject of his father, because in the context of unhappiness and depression his father would only comment, "Just get a grip John." Fortunately for John he didn't go any further than that. He had gained enough realisations as it was.

Now with these sorts of realisations three things could occur: the first - that his defence mechanism comes in and blocks off his thoughts and feelings, the second - he could become emotionally upset, and the third - he could become angry. The first two would result in a passive state; with the first one nothing will change, with the second, after a period when the emotions calm down, the first state might enter or he would start to think about how to change things. In the third state he could react and that reaction would go towards his mother. John, not being adept as yet with the second floor consciousness, was becoming angry and was choosing to react. We will take up once more with his thinking processes.

"That's it," he thought. "I am going to tell her what I think, I have never done that, but I have had enough. She's ruined my life long enough, it's got to stop. As soon as I get home I'm getting on the phone." Obviously you couldn't blame John for thinking all this, but a reaction to a realisation such as this could well turn out to be a disaster. John would do better to allow his anger to subside and think from a place of emotional calm about what to do to change the situation. John has started to change but his mother hasn't, and she is a very strong Bastian of self-idealism indoctrinated by some very strange religious beliefs, in short she is always right.

Now his entire focus was to address the situation, but he was still aware, as the first encounter earlier in the day with the silence proved to him, the need not to drive as he felt. Finally arriving home he switched off the engine, fumbling for his keys he leapt out of the car straight into a pile of dog poo, unfortunately it wasn't that old.

"It's that *@@"!!**@ dog next door." His thoughts were interrupted by the sudden activation of his sense of smell. "Oh shit!" he thought, how apt. Opening the front door, quickly he kicked his shoes off into the drive. Of course John still was wearing those socks from this morning which obviously his shoes had worked well to contain the smell. Now I think John could have just coped with that, but he was wondering why his sense of smell still contained the essence of the dog poo, the answer soon came - it was on his sock, when he kicked off his shoes, he accidentally smudged the sticky poo from his shoe across his sock. All thoughts about ringing his mother had disappeared, as he was now confronted with a tricky situation. He had gone several steps into his hallway, looking back, to his horror, there on his carpet were beautifully spaced brown dabs, he looked at them then looked at his sock. He became in total vibration with the space and situation.

"What the F**! do I do now?" thought John. Well, the intellectual approach would be to take the socks off first, "Good idea," he thought. He leaned against the wall with one hand and removed the poo covered sock first, this obviously was an instinctual reaction based upon the circumstance, because he now had the problem of removing the other one. The simple answer would have been to have carried the sock into the kitchen and out of the back door and into the dustbin, but unfortunately John's thinking was in disarray. The second floor thinking was starting to enter, therefore certain aspects of the first floor thinking, for example the ability to have rationally worked out the problem he now had, (which one could easily visualise at this moment with a sense of humour which John, regarding this situation, does not possess) so these practicalities tend to initially leave the consciousness, until a certain amount of the new way of thinking can enter, to then bring back this intellectual approach – but, even better than before. So to his mind he was confronted with the fact of removing the other sock whilst holding suitably away from himself the poo riddled sock, which was starting, so the speak, to "get up his nose."

He decided to sit down by using his other hand on the wall to lower himself down. Now the sock was in his right hand

and came off his right foot, he soon realised he couldn't remove his left foot sock with his left hand, so he transferred the offending sock to his left hand to tackle the left foot with his right hand, after a bit of an effort he was successful, and then with a blur of speed he was out of the back door finally placing them firmly in the bin.

Let us look at this incident, bearing in mind there are no coincidences. Did some divine power impress the dog to poo in exactly the right place for when John returned home, knowing that this would avert the big mistake he was going to make with his mother? Or did the second floor consciousness impress John to park exactly in the right place for this to happen? There is a cliché that is banded around in the conversations of those aspiring towards the spiritual path; "It was meant to be." Well, in this context I don't think John would have gone along with that, and in a way it does tend to avoid issues. But one thing is certain, it stopped him from phoning his mother and sometimes it is well just to accept circumstance rather than to delve too deeply into the happenings of the day.

He entered back into the kitchen, shutting and locking the back door, then just stood there for a moment trying to regain his capacity to think. "I need a shower," he thought. Making sure the hot water was on, he was magnetically drawn towards the fridge and that wasn't for food. Who could blame anyone for not wanting any food after that, no, he rapidly removed a bottle of beer and within the same movement plucked a bottle opener out of the drawer and removed the top. Then all became still and silent, no this wasn't another case of the second floor trying to impress him, it was the moment just before he drank the beer, you could call it a moment of anticipation. He took a couple of swigs, drew a breath, and sighed, "What a day," he thought and then rushed upstairs for his shower which was sorely needed.

As he started to relax the hot water washed away his stress and tension, his thoughts went to what Linda was saying about meditation and the group Miranda was running. "I know," he thought, "I'll Google meditation and healing and see what it is all about." Feeling somewhat cleaner John descended, the first port of call was the bottle of beer, then the computer. John had heard something from Linda concerning the New Age, so he Googled 'Meditation, Healing and New Age'. He would have been better off leaving out the words New Age as what then confronted him as he trawled through the sites was an incomprehensible mixture of, by analogy, 'Star Trek' and 'Religious Practice'.

"I don't understand all this," John thought, followed by, "Is this what they are into?" He scribbled a few things down and decided to go to bed. He lay in bed, the whole day seemed to run through his head and when he finally caught up with himself he fell asleep.

Two Weeks Later:

The alarm clock shrills its message into the space, the room resounds to its repetitive sound growing louder by the second, a hand reaches out and misses the clock knocking it over a grunt-like sound was heard, as John rolled out of bed in pursuit of the alarm clock he had knocked across the wooden floor. The sound abruptly comes to an end. John had made it out of bed, the covers of his bed in a dishevelled heap, John paused trying to achieve some sort of brain consciousness. "Ha," he thought, "it's Friday!" Before he could become too happy about this prospect, another thought came to him, it then dawned on him that it was Wednesday.

At that point some sort of déjà vu entered his head, "I remember all this from a few weeks ago," he thought, "It's not going to be one of those days is it?" Now John's habit of cutting things fine had changed slightly in two weeks, his alarm clock was now set fifteen minutes earlier, but yes, there it was, the shirt that he was going to iron the night before lay on the floor in a crinkled mess. The extra time he had given himself allowed for this situation, therefore, so far there have been no obscenities spoken. Well done John, he had obviously learned a lesson. It had taken twenty years but then some people never learn it and continue to blame some invisible person for their misfortune or even worse, their wife or husband. John quickly ironed his shirt without any undue stress, still feeling a little strange that this had all happened before and it had, two weeks ago. Then it suddenly dawned upon John the sequence of events, and that involved his socks, for a brief moment he couldn't move.

"Surely I haven't done the same thing?" he rushed to his sock drawer then paused hardly daring to open it just in case it was *empty*. He plucked up courage and there in the drawer, feeling pretty lonely, was a clean pair of socks. "Phew!" he thought, "I've averted that one." He picked up his socks in such a way as if they were a friend and of course they were. He had lost some time ironing his shirt but he was still on schedule. John was now working *with* time. "Lunch" he thought as he threw open the fridge door, there was a little bit more choice, as John, maybe to an extent subconsciously, had decided to add more variety to his eating habits. He had not spoken to his mother for a while and there was now not a need to rebel against her opinions, so John this time was not confronted by his duality, well not regarding his food. He packed his lunch quickly feeling very pleased with himself, things were going far better than two weeks previously.

Now the interesting thing when acquiring a new found awareness, is that it is not that simple, life doesn't instantly become a *breeze*. Because what happens is, there will occur some sort of challenge regarding this. John had overcome the influence of his mother regarding her control on him in certain areas of his life, and in this case it was food, but then he hadn't seen or spoken to her, therefore he had created the space to allow him to work it all out. Very commendable John, but these challenges always appear when you least expect them.

John was heading for the front door totally relaxed when the phone rang. Now there is such a thing as discrimination, he could have let it go to answerphone, this discrimination thing was John's next lesson. Without thinking he picked it up.

"Hello John," said his mother. "I thought I would catch you before you went to work." He had been caught all right, John froze, his feeling very pleased with himself disintegrated at the speed of light.

"Have you been avoiding me John?" said his mother.

"No," said John "I've been really busy."

"Anyway, I have something for you, John. Can you come round later to pick it up? I would be so pleased to see you, I have felt a bit lonely recently and you would cheer me up, is that OK?"

Before he could think he said one word "Yes." Before he could reverse his stupidity his mother had instantly put the phone down. John stood there holding the phone in some sort of trance, then it dawned on him, he had arranged to meet Linda later. He had arranged that two weeks ago. He quickly put the phone down as he also realised he might now be late for work, no time to phone her back now.

"I'll sort it out later," he thought. He rushed out the door and jumped into his car. He threw his engine into rapid life, revved it up and rammed it into gear. "Hang on," he thought, "this is where it all started." He paused, looked out of his window to see a woman walk past with a dog. "Something strange is happening here," and then the silence came over him.

Over the two weeks he had almost forgotten about it although slight changes had happened to him in the way he thought and felt. He sat with the silence for a couple of minutes until he noticed the time which magnified itself in front of his eyes. He pulled off the drive on his journey to work which was still the same route every day. Aware of the time he was beginning to feel slightly stressed, the traffic lights were not being very kind to him, so he was faced with the same challenge as two weeks ago. He was starting to think, if he hadn't answered the phone he wouldn't be in this predicament, also he could have avoided meeting his mother this evening. Now would he learn from this or put himself down and start repeating the same patterns? He was starting to put himself down when the car in front decided to commit an act of goodwill by letting the car out of a side street into the main flow of traffic. Was John going to react to this, throwing internal abuse or maybe external abuse at the driver in front, which wouldn't exactly create a harmonious atmosphere in the car? John was starting to realise about atmospheres, but as yet could not apply this concept to himself too much. His opportunity will come for him to realise how his thoughts and feelings can affect other people. Very commendable, John. He didn't bat an eye, but then he hadn't noticed the car that was let out of the side street, he was too busy in thought and sometimes thought can inhibit sight. He did though start to wonder why he had slowed down, the car in front of him suddenly turned left and there it was, in front of him was a learner driver. John immediately looked at the clock with his brain rapidly computing the situation. Now what brain was he using to do this, his first floor brain or the same brain influenced by the second floor? He entered a little bit of a battle with these two aspects of himself and just as the second floor influence was starting to win, he noticed it was the same learner driver as it was two weeks ago.

We pause at this moment to see which way he will go, we didn't have to wait too long.

John was starting to sink into his old self, although not that old as it has only been two weeks. Off he went with a stream of abuse, "Just get out of my @@'""*!@ way," he thought as he started to fumble for his cigarette packet. Out came a cigarette grabbing his lighter he clicked it down, it didn't work. "Oh shit" he thought, "plenty of fuel," but unfortunately a tiny piece of tissue had lodged itself on top of the nozzle. Bear in mind while all this was happening John was still driving. So there he was blowing the tissue out of his lighter and clicking it down again when the learner driver did an emergency stop, we are not sure exactly why, but it could have been because a pigeon was in the road. John's reflexes were brilliant, but unfortunately he had just lit his lighter and as he lurched forward he singed his eyebrow, John was not quite aware of this until he smelt a distinct burnt smell. "Oh *@!*" he thought. He pulled over to check himself in the mirror. Yes, his eyebrow was slightly charred, sitting back he suddenly realised his attitude was the same as two weeks ago.

"Surely my attitude didn't cause this to happen again?" Unfortunately things have a nasty habit of repeating themselves, it relates to what is known as cause and effect. Now, because John has started to become impressed by the second floor consciousness, he has entered into a rapid learning process which requires him to change his attitude. Some people may never change their attitude so they will stay within the first floor consciousness until a tap upon the consciousness occurs. It is trying to register what it is trying to say, and life's circumstances and events will give a clue.

This time John was starting to see the light, and as we said, there are no coincidences. He composed himself and drove the rest of the way to work with no further problems, also with a few minutes to spare. He strode into work and arrived at his desk, but felt a strange atmosphere, not dissimilar to two weeks ago. But John was a little bit more aware now and looked around the room. Jane didn't look right and Trevor was distinctly upset. John was starting to observe now on an energetic level. People's problems can be felt, but also their demeanour can reveal a lot, even if they are trying not to display their problems. This was quite understandable as this office requires that problems with the staff do not exist as it will appear as a weakness in the team. But John was starting to care about people, he saw Jane at the coffee machine and something inspired him to go over.

"Hello Jane, are you all right? You don't seem yourself recently." John's tone of voice reflected his compassion and compassion comes from the second floor consciousness. Jane tried to pretend everything was all right, but as she looked at John's eyes, she couldn't hold back her feelings, she started to tell John her worries about her father, her voice suddenly broke up as the tears started to fill in her eyes.

John said, "It's all right Jane, I understand. I am here for you if you need me." She couldn't contain herself any longer and started to cry. John held her in his arms with a feeling of compassion; she stopped crying and composed herself, looked around to see if anybody had noticed.

"Thank you John, I will be all right now." And she walked away to her desk. John thought while he was there, a coffee would be nice. Just as the cup had filled John felt a presence behind him. It was Trevor. John hadn't quite learned the art of diplomacy especially concerning his newfound art of observation.

"Are you all right Trevor? You look like I did when my wife was having a go at me; anyway we have split up now." Trevor's face was a picture and suddenly John had realised he had hit a home truth. "Oh no," thought John, "I have really put my foot in it."

John's speech stumbled as he tried to say sorry to Trevor, but he wasn't doing a very good job. Sometimes it is best not to back pedal as it can make things worse, and it did. Trevor was starting to get angry. "Need to divert this" thought John. "How about a drink, Trevor?"

"Thanks," said Trevor, "coffee with two sugars," his face was like stone. John popped his money into the machine and pressed the buttons. Cups are automatically dispensed from the machine and John had forgotten to remove his coffee, down came the cup followed quickly by the coffee. John's coffee went flying, he tried to catch it and burnt his fingers. What a mess!

Trevor's face started to change and he suddenly broke down in hysterical laughter - we think it was a release from all the stress he was suffering, in fact, he couldn't stop and every time he looked at John it got worse. "Well at least he's not angry anymore," thought John.

Was this divine intervention or just the result of John getting worried about Trevor's reaction to his comments and forgetting to move his cup? Whatever, it broke the ice and John, so to speak, got away with it. But the incident was attracting a bit of an audience in the office and the laughter became infectious, so much so it attracted the manager's attention, probably not a good start to the day attracting her attention.

Helen was feeling particularly mean as she had just been informed that she was going to have to attend a health and safety course involving written reports, etc. Now Helen couldn't exactly tell the managing director what she thought about the prospect as Helen was also seeking promotion. So the energy of her conflict had not been expressed; but what can happen then is that somebody else gets it. Now Helen is a control freak, that is why she is manager and in this case she has no control. John with his newfound perception immediately picked up something was wrong with Helen. Her anger preceded her at a great distance. The office fell into silence, even Trevor managed to control himself. "This needs some quick thinking," thought John. "Good morning Helen. I was just discussing a brand new revolutionary sales approach with Trevor and got so involved I forgot to take my coffee out."

Now the response of the office and Trevor to this incident was probably due to the spectre of redundancy that was still circulating. One wonders whether this was just a managerial tactic to keep the staff on their toes.

John defused Helen beautifully. She suddenly took no notice of the mess at all.

"That sounds interesting, I have half an hour free this afternoon, you can discuss this with me then." and she walked away.

Trevor looked at John, "Is that true John or were you making it up to stop the old dog from barking at you?"

John had gone into Trevor mode with a face of stone, he clicked out of it. "I didn't think she would want to discuss it, she never has in the past," but then John was doing very well with his sales, hence Helen *was* interested.

"By the way," said Trevor "you were right. I have a lot of problems with my wife at the moment. I am trying to be all right at work because I don't want it to affect my colleagues, it's my problem not theirs, but it's not looking very good. Anyway, it's probably not as bad as the problem you might have with Helen this afternoon."

And just to rub it in, Linda came over. "That was very lucky John, looking forward to this evening." And walked away.

John was left standing by the coffee machine with a mess to clear up, a problem with three people, and he hadn't even started working yet. He was just about to panic when the silence came in on him and he started to tell himself, in his head, to do things one at a time: first tackle the mess, start working, try to get mother during the break, and the problem with Helen will sort itself out during the day and you will know what to do. This was guidance from the second floor, but with the last bit concerning Helen it takes a lot of trust, trust that the right answers will come. The 'first floor John' would now be panicking trying to formulate all sorts of ways to clear himself, but the 'second floor John' was, at this moment, in charge once more. A single word came into his head "Truth", and this you need to remember John told himself.

With the mess cleared up John finally made his desk, the phone immediately rang, it was the customer from two weeks previous, you remember the one he gave the discount to which then gained him a very large order. Since then John has never looked back, because he has found that if he does his best for his customers, forgetting about his own gain, then he automatically gains as a result, this he has achieved through "Truth." He immediately made the connection. John was also far more relaxed with his customers and they felt this, so the conversation was quite light hearted. It was quite a large order when it finally came around to it, but there was a slight snag. They wanted it first thing in the morning, less than 24 hours delivery, and the order depended on it.

They normally deliver in two to three working days, more like three really. Now the reasons for this are varied but essentially it all comes down to money, John had been seeing this as a problem. Then before he could think he came straight out with it, "That's not a problem, it will be there by 9 a.m. on the dot."

John had taken it upon himself to change the company policy and of course he hadn't consulted Helen. He put the phone down, pondered briefly, then decided instead of the usual red-tape and paperwork, he phoned the order to the warehouse telling them the paperwork would follow. There was some resistance but John was very much in control and he was quite amazing considering what he used to be like. They agreed.

"Now for someone to deliver it." He was on the phone like lightning collating the options, he secured the delivery with quite a new company, obviously they wanted the business (like all the others) but they seemed very truthful about the delivery, they weren't the cheapest.

"All sorted," he thought. It was break time. "Now for mother." Unfortunately he couldn't get her, but then he wasn't going to, she was a bit cleverer than John about answering the phone. "I'll try again at lunch time" he thought.

John then sorted the paperwork and the phone rang. Another customer and, guess what, they wanted a fast delivery. John had broken the block that was restricting his sales - although he was still doing well. Now this second customer knew nothing about John changing the policy, but then here we see the Law of Attraction. John had set something in motion and through a vast connectivity he had a response. This also was a large order, he organised the delivery once more using diverse methods and fast tracking the order without the paperwork.

Now in this day and age of rules and order, this is starting to be unheard of. John was thinking for himself not from the restrictions placed upon him, and he was loving it. Lunch time was approaching. Linda called over.

"Don't forget the relaxation class with Miranda."

John had almost forgotten, as the last one was two weeks previous, he started to remember what happened before and Miranda's words that had stuck with him, "Don't worry John, I understand." John had also used these words himself to his ex-wife and a couple of other people. He also recalled the incident with the socks, which actually now he could laugh about, this proves that John's confidence had grown.

Anyway, five minutes till lunch time, but enough time for one more call, it was a quote. John had developed the art of working the quote out whilst talking to the customer, therefore you could say he was multitasking, and as we all know men are probably not so good at that. He delivered a keen price, but John knew this customer played the quoting game and normally John can miss out with someone just undercutting him. So at the end of the quote, he threw in his Ace card, "Oh, by the way, I can deliver it for you tomorrow before 12 noon, you could have it on the shelf by the following day's opening." There was a brief silence, you could almost hear his customer's brain ticking over.

"That's an interesting proposition John, I think I will go for that." John scored a third success. He was feeling quite good and then it dawned on him, he still had the problem of his mother, which then gave him a problem with Linda. "I'll try and get her after the class, she is always in at that time." Knowing that relieved some sort of pressure off of John, but then the pressure came back when he remembered what Helen had said, and of course what John had said to Helen to initiate her response.

Let us revisit this. "Good morning Helen I was just discussing a brand new revolutionary sales approach with Trevor." And her response "That sounds interesting I have half an hour spare this afternoon for you to discuss this with me." Pausing, John looked into the space of the room, all outer noise seemed to quieten, John was realising when this happened he gained insight, and he did. "Wait a moment," he thought, "perhaps I already have the basis of a revolutionary new sales technique," and the words 'Truth' and 'Trust' came into his mind. Also his method of fast delivery and quick quoting and his very integrated approach with no expectations.

He was jolted out of the silence by Trevor. "Come on," he said, "we are the last ones, everyone else is already at the class." And he rushed off.

John approached the room, he was looking forward to seeing Miranda again. He had some sort of resonance with her, he wasn't quite sure what it was. "Maybe because she understood," he thought, but it could be more than that.

Miranda was at the doorway. "Hello John, lovely to see you again, we are just about to start." There was a brief moment when their eyes met.

"Sorry I'm late." He walked into the room in a slight trance almost falling over himself, something had happened to John when he looked into Miranda's eyes. He sat down and the session started. He noticed there was a carrier bag in the corner. "Thank God I haven't got last time's problem," he thought.

Miranda gave a talk about the centres of consciousness and their relationship to health and how meditation can bring about a positive effect upon them. John was fascinated, he had never heard of them. Then Miranda said one thing that John could relate to, she said, "and these centres, when in balance, bring about a silence, a moment of calm within chaos, allowing you to go to the centre of the circle." John immediately related this to those silent moments he had experienced. "I need to know more about this" he thought.

Miranda mixed some very simple Yoga with relaxation techniques, finishing with a meditation. It was in that meditation that John started to experience things happening.

With his eyes closed he saw colours moving and changing, and at one point a bright white light. Words came into his head, they were the same words as earlier, Truth and Trust, but he also got the words "you have to be your true self." The meditation was finished but John was deep in thought, people started to leave, eventually he was the only one there other than Miranda.

"Are you all right John?" John hadn't moved, his eyes were open but he was somewhat bowled over by the experience.

"Err, yes" he replied and stood up and centred himself. "That was unbelievable." He blurted out a couple of things. "But I haven't got time to tell you everything. I need to gain some understanding as I think this is connected to what is going on in my life."

"Why don't you ring me later? I am busy up until 9.30 p.m. so after that would be good, but no later than 10 p.m., is all right?" and she gave John her card.

John, still not quite fully present, said he would ring. "And by the way, what you said to me last time has really made quite a difference to me, nobody has ever said that."

Miranda knew what she had said and suddenly felt a real compassion for John, even more so when she noticed a tear in the corner of one of his eyes, it started to roll down his cheek. John instantly wiped it away, he couldn't be that open with someone, Miranda was quite aware that John was trying to mask his emotions.

"I'll speak to you later then John." She then gave John a hug with every intention of withdrawing, but she didn't and nor did John, something that most people never experience. They were like two magnets unable to separate, each one experiencing the other in warmth and a flow of energy that gave to each a wonderful sensation of lovingness. It could have lasted a lifetime. John gently moved his hands across Miranda's back; Miranda responded. This became a miracle of relationship whereby both felt the ultimate sensation of belonging and the flow of love, all this from a hug. It naturally came to an end, as they parted and looked at each other; both were speechless. There was nothing of a sexual nature here, it is possible to hug someone in that way without those sorts of expectations or feelings.

John broke the silence, as in the deep recesses of his consciousness, he was aware he had to go back to work. "I'll ring you later if that's all right. Time to go to work," and he walked back into the office leaving Miranda standing there.

No, nobody saw them hug, but maybe John's demeanour and auric vibrations were telling a story, and people pick up on that sort of thing very easily, therefore John was getting some funny, almost I-know-what's-just-happened looks. He arrived back at his desk; all sorts of things were running through his mind. "What the hell happened there?" he thought. "That was unbelievable. What do I do about it and what do I say to Miranda tonight if she asks?"

John was still reliving the experience, then suddenly his brain cells went into total recoil. "I haven't spoken to my mother yet." He quickly whisked out his mobile phone, now if that was a six-gun he would have been the fastest draw in the wild-west. Up came his mother's number, a press of the finger and her phone was ringing.

John composed himself and suddenly realised that he hadn't formulated what he was going to say. "Oh no, I need to think quickly!" but then something quietened him down and in his head came the words "Why don't you tell her the truth?"

"But that will then lead to an interrogation as to who Linda was and everything about her, as mother doesn't leave any stone unturned."

"You could take control of that John, instead of just going along with what she wants to hear, don't give your power away."

Anyway, the phone just rang and rang. His mother didn't have an answering machine, she didn't believe in that sort of thing. It is a miracle she actually has a phone, but then she couldn't get hold of John, 'get hold of' being the operative words. John's stomach fell to the floor, realising he was getting deeper in the *!!*.

"That's bloody great! What do I do now?" he ended the call. "I don't think she is going to answer me just in case I cancel. Perhaps I need to interact with my mother in a different manner. There needs to be a different approach."

John is right, he does need to change the way he interacts, then his mother might change the way she talks and interacts with John. There is a tendency to fall into patterns of behaviour, and sometimes these are developed at a very early age and become perpetuated, whereby each party cannot break the pattern. John has already gained a clue to this and that is truth. John also needs to open his emotions and feelings to his mother, he is very blocked on that level and adopts a defence mechanism. The result of this is his mother tries to break down his defences to get a response, and of course, she doesn't - therefore she tries even harder. Where does all this leave John? Well, he feels he is being criticised, and of course this feeling of criticism can become exacerbated within his other interactions, leading to a lack of self-confidence and an over sensitivity, but always finding it hard to display any feeling. Well, these barriers seem to be falling down, he certainly felt something with Miranda. This is related to the opening of the heart centre, this is a second floor activity and of course, this doesn't just extend itself to one person or the necessity to hug someone, it is more than that. One word we could use is 'compassion' and when you take yourself away from yourself as being the centre of the universe, then you can appreciate other people's difficulties from that place of compassion.

Now John has another word and that is 'Trust'. He is starting to trust himself, his trust in others is very limited due to his experiences. But John also has obtained the word 'discrimination' which becomes a working partnership with 'trust' and that will lead you to the truth of the matter. At the moment John is now seriously thinking about that, and has decided it is no good continually trying to avoid his mother, he needs to change the dynamics of their relationship.

"But how am I going to do it?" he thought. "Firstly, I need to drop my defence mechanism. Be truthful, add some joy to our interactions and try to understand her."

Now bear in mind John is still pivoting between his first floor consciousness and second floor consciousness, therefore he will probably argue with himself, and the first floor consciousness puts up a good argument, which it did. Backwards and forwards he went.

Let us bring an analogy here by placing the word backwards with the first floor consciousness and forwards with the second floor consciousness. It is all too easy to rotate back into existing thought and feeling, as it has been a resident within the consciousness and will automatically, out of the blue, rise up and install itself once more into outer appearance. The second floor consciousness is new and leads you into slightly uncharted waters, in short it takes away what people call the comfort blanket, and of course you cannot know how much more there is to this state of consciousness until you start to arrive at it. Now John could have been stuck with this for quite a while, but something else entered into this contest. This something comes from the third floor and this third floor encompasses the other two.

We shall see if it has an effect upon John. Is he ready for this?

It was just like a switch was thrown and John's mind instantly moved from the problem of his mother to the impending problem of Helen, the manager.

"What was the time?" Now John knew she couldn't possibly be free until 3 p.m. "It's 2 p.m., I have an hour to come up with something." John normally takes days to present something to Helen, constantly altering his presentation so it would please her, and of course, it very rarely did. John's focus was on pleasing Helen, not upon any of his creative ideas or indeed truth, and John had had a lot of creative ideas but had done nothing about them, until now. Creative ideas come from the second floor consciousness, so John was in touch with this, but didn't know it. Now today John was slightly impressed with the third floor consciousness because he had put into action his creative ideas. So here we are, can he in one short hour, barring any phone calls, put something together for Helen? Had he enough confidence to do this? He flashed his computer into action, opened a new document and typed inadvertently 'this is the day I take control of my life'. Looking at the blank page, nothing came. He spotted a pen beside his computer. He decided he needed some fresh air to clear his head, he picked up the pen not knowing why, John had always used the computer. He also picked up a small note pad and went outside looking for a suitable place to hide so he could light up. An idea popped into his mind. He went around the side of the building and sat on the grass. His idea started to take shape and the stillness then entered, as he stared at the space in front of him he became aware that this silence and space gave him ideas. The smoke from his cigarette glided gently across his vision, there was a brief moment and then he went into action and started to write his ideas as they came into his head, he was having trouble keeping up with their content, writing as fast as he could.

"This is unbelievable" he thought as he continued writing. There was a couple of pauses as John's intellectual mind started to analyse the content and formulate it. Fortunately John became aware of this and relegated his intellectual mind into the background, using it only to transpose the words that were coming into his head, until it abruptly finished and nothing else came in. He had completely written his presentation in simplistic form in fifteen minutes.

John had just learned something else about the silence. He had realised the space and timelessness, and that if you are searching for ideas, the silence will give you them. This is another aspect of the second floor consciousness: ideas. Many would think "Where do they come from then? Are they just floating in space?" because the interesting thing, John's ideas, hadn't come from a book. These ideas from the silence are intangible, they become tangible if you have a positive purpose for them. OK, this purpose is related to sales, which you could say is materialistic in nature, but John is bringing in two aspects related to the second floor. Truth and Trust, therefore the second floor has responded in John's hour of need because, as mentioned before, John has something to do in this life.

He arrived back at his desk so fast as if he had been teleported there and began to type, filling in the details. That took him 20 minutes, he saved the document, printed it and then bound it up. John sat at his desk looking at his document. "My goodness, how did I do that?" Flicking through it, he thought "This is the best thing I have ever done," and a smile came over his face. This was becoming more of a regular occurrence. And then in his moment of triumph, his first floor consciousness came in, a dark cloud entered his mind. He also remembered that part of what he was presenting he had already implemented, his breathing quickened and he started to feel hot.

"She will never go with this." There was a tap on his shoulder, it was Linda.

"You all right John?" She noticed his document. "Do you mind if I read it?" she said.

"No," said John as he had entered into a statue state. John waited for Linda to comment, watching her facial expressions to see if she approved, and then she looked at John. There was a pause.

"This is brilliant, John. Just what this company needs. You need to believe in yourself, some things are just a stepping stone." And she walked away.

John was puzzled. What did she mean by stepping stone? Did she mean the document? Before he could think further on this his phone rang. It was Helen.

"Hello John. Come to my office so we can discuss your revolutionary new sales technique."

John really wished he had not said that, but then sometimes what may appear to be a mistake from a first floor level, is not from a second floor level, as the second floor consciousness is more expansive and is progressive. Look at what has come from what John had wished he hadn't said.

"I'll be there in two minutes," said John, he put the phone down in slow motion. He was quite calm, a bit like a prisoner who has accepted he is in jail, and then Linda's words came into him mind. "You need to believe in yourself," then something happened - he did. In fact, he got quite excited about presenting his document, obviously forgetting it was to Helen, and off he went to her office.

The office door was open. "Come in," said Helen, "have a seat." For one brief moment she sounded like his mother. This could have completely blown it for him, but he immediately centred himself and sat down.

"OK John. What have you got?" Now John had not formulated his approach, so he could not intellectually proceed in any logical sequence. He had his document but that needed explaining. He handed Helen a copy, fortunately he had produced two. This gave him a moment while Helen briefly glanced at it.

"You will need to explain this, John."

"OK. I will start with the concept of truth, as I see this relating to a highly productive form of interactive selling whereby the client engages in having his needs met through the element of trust." There was a stunned silence from Helen. Was John really saying this? Yes he was, this is his second floor consciousness and that works if you believe in yourself. John proceeded from there explaining the practicalities of his presentation, concluding with his method of fast delivery by bypassing existing procedures and paperwork, seeing the paperwork as a necessity but not as a restriction for improving the speed of delivery and then he finished, waiting for a response.

Now Helen's facial expression is always the same, so you cannot tell whether she likes something or not. The time John had to wait was probably only a minute, but my God it seemed like ten to him. Her eyes looked straight into his. John, in the past, would have been intimidated by this, but not this time. He believed in himself and his ideas. Helen chose her words, she obviously thought this was worthwhile, "This is very interesting John. There are certain methods I can add to this." What she was saying was that this was not going to be all John's work, and any credit for it was actually going to her, not John. "As for the delivery aspect, which we could, as you have pointed out, improve, but bypassing paperwork, that is against company policy and cannot be considered."

John's brain went into overdrive. "But I already have," he thought. He could have lost it at this point but he was still within the second floor consciousness and replied, "What if it was proven to be the obstacle for us increasing sales, and our inability to give next day delivery, because of the paperwork, caused clients to use another supplier? I propose this is the case."

"Have you done a summary then, John?"

"No," replied John.

"So what do you base your statement upon?" Now John had to be up-front with the fact that he had already initiated this and so he explained this to Helen. A silence followed. Well not quite, as a fly started to buzz around John's head. He tried to ignore it, but it began settling on him. Waving his arms to discourage this annoying fly, he accidentally clipped the glass of water on the office table and down it went, all over the floor, but not an ordinary floor. Helen had a brand new carpet, to reflect her sense of power, which blended beautifully with the new office furniture. Now it could have been worse, it could have been coffee, just like what had happened this morning which caused John to be sitting there now. John jumped up apologising and went for the paper towel to clean it up. In one way it had caused a diversion which had thrown Helen off course. He cleared it up quickly.

"I'll talk to you later," said Helen and left her office leaving John standing there with a pile of wet paper towels in his hand.

"Not sure whether that went well, or not," he thought and went back to his desk.

A couple of organised phone calls later, John was left with the problem of his mother. "A cup of coffee," he thought. He stood waiting for his coffee, watching it going into his cup when he heard Linda's voice. He was in a little bit of a world of his own, he turned and saw Linda. The automatic response was "Like a coffee, Linda?"

"Thanks, John." As he put the money in, some sort of déjà vu came over him and he carefully removed his cup of coffee.

"Not long before we can go out," she said. John has based his presentation or part of it upon Truth, which now he needed to use in this situation with Linda.

"Can I have a word with you, Linda? I have a problem."

"Fine, John."

He explained to her the predicament he was in and that he didn't know what to do. "I really want to go out with you, Linda, but I can't because of my mother. She caught me on the hop this morning and I promised to see her, and in some way I need to resolve my problem with her."

Linda looked at John and she understood what he was saying because Linda was in touch with the second floor consciousness, therefore she was not selfish even though she was really looking forward to going out with John.

"What time are you seeing her?"

"Straight after work."

"Why don't you see me after that? Put a time limit on your visit to an hour and I'll meet you at the pub after that, say 7.30 p.m.?"

John thought about that very deeply, this is different. He started to warm to the idea, he had never done that before, but if he did it would change the dynamics. But his mother is very powerful on an energetic level and for some reason after about ten minutes, John feels drained and unable to stand his ground, but maybe he doesn't need to stand his ground, just be truthful, this is where the challenge lies. His mother isn't powerful as in physically strong, that would conjure up an image. No, she wants more from John than he is prepared to give, therefore the energy of her words carry the frequency of her desire which then plays out upon John. This he is starting to understand. Maybe along with truth, John needs to give his mother compassion without any fear of rejection, and this issue of rejection has also contributed to John's defence mechanism.

"That's a good idea, Linda," and then he suddenly remembered the phone call with Miranda. He paused, "but I have to be home by 9.30 p.m. I have an important phone call to make."

Linda noticed a slight smile on John's face. She smiled, "It looks important to me, I won't ask who to. See you later then" and she walked away.

"Oh well, never a dull moment," he thought. John cleared up all the paperwork from the orders earlier and put them neatly in a pile. He was slightly preoccupied whilst he did this and was not quite aware of his surroundings. He was jolted into reality.

"Is that the paperwork for the orders, John?" asked Helen. He hadn't noticed her.

"Err, yes," he said.

"Thank you, I'll take these then," said Helen and walked away.

"How strange," John thought, "but maybe this is a good sign." He looked at his watch, five minutes to finish time and he tidied up his desk. Looks like a busy evening.

A train of thought entered his head, "Just be yourself John, why don't you try and enjoy it all?"

"Why not?" he thought. Lifting his eyebrows he smiled. "I need to stop worrying."

John was adopting a positive attitude and the key words were 'enjoy it all'. To enjoy, to experience joy, this is a major shift in consciousness. It releases one from doubt, guilt and many other personal experiences and it is according to how we approach these experiences, as to what the experience will deliver, and the word *all* meaning all levels of experience, even those that are most physical in nature. So, John is now going to deliver joy.

He finds himself driving down the small lane towards his mother's house and actually looking forward to seeing her.

He had, to a degree, self-induced some of that. He turned right into the drive. The outside light came on and then he felt the tension increase, his sub-conscious memory was triggering it, just like the feelings he got on every visit. Why were these coming in as he was so positive? Well, if an experience repeats itself, it becomes a pattern and that pattern can bring about the feelings concerning the pattern - just by being in the environment of what created it. He pulled up on the drive feeling extremely anxious. He realised what was happening.

"These are the feelings I normally get." His mind had grasped the concept of Miranda's meditations and relaxation; he quietly went through a relaxation and to his surprise, he went back to how he was before he had arrived. "That was bloody good," he thought. "Let's get this over with," and he remembered the concept of an hour. He jumped out of the car and approached the front door which miraculously opened, the light poured out from inside the house, and there silhouetted in the doorway, was his mother.

"Hello, John. What were you doing in the car?"

John felt his defence come up, "oh I did a quick relaxation, it's been a busy day."

"I suppose the next thing you'll be doing is meditation, what a load of old rubbish. Come in."

John's mind started to analyse that statement, a normal response from his mind would be, "that's bloody typical." Now the sentence itself, possibly removing the middle word, is not a problem if thought about by the higher consciousness as an observation, particularly with a sense of humour. But otherwise, from a negative point of view, the vibration of that statement would carry an energy that would trigger many other negative statements that reside within John's memory, thus increasing the potentiality for a downward spiral into a state of negativity and his old patterns of behaviour. So it is at this point now whether John will proceed still in the state of positivity.

"Yes," John adopted a sense of humour to his inner thought.

They sat down and John took the lead. "I have an hour mother, let's make the most of it. What have you bought me?" Smiling he quickly stopped himself from saying "How are you?" otherwise that could have been a disaster.

For once his mother stumbled, it took her by surprise. To her John is normally so miserable, to John she is always so dictatorial and critical. Perhaps each state is based upon each other's disposition.

"Err yes, I'll give it to you in a minute," before she could say another word John started to converse and talk about his day with creative expression and humour, which he never did, and slowly his mother started to smile. Her own tension disappeared and a small tear formed in the corner of her eye. Her criticism disappeared and she was really enjoying what John was saying, so much so that she started to cry. John had never seen his mother show any emotion, he suddenly started to have feelings for her and he went over and put his arm around her.

"Mother, I understand, let me make you a cup of tea."

"Thank you John." He took the tea in and his mother was holding a photograph and tears were rolling down her face.

"I was never going to tell you this, John," and in a brief moment John had realised why his mother never showed any emotion. She had locked something away for a long time. It was a picture of two babies, twins. She looked directly at John, "That's you, John."

"What does this mean?" thought John, as he felt a nervousness in his stomach.

"And that's James."

"What happened to James?" thought John.

"He died I'm afraid, John." And then it all made sense. A tear then rolled down John's cheek.

.His mother stood up "I'm sorry for being so hard on you," there was a pause "I put all my expectations upon you as a means of overcoming my grief."

He swiftly stood up and took his mother in his arms, nothing was said. After a while they sat down. John said with deep concern, "I have to go now mother, will you be alright?"

"Yes, I will, but can I speak to you tomorrow?" Her face had transformed and was kind of soft looking.

"But of course," said John and left.

He pulled off the drive and made his way to the pub to meet Linda. He felt like a great weight had been lifted off him, but also there was a sense of sadness with what his mother had told him. It only took 20 minutes to reach the pub. It was most peculiar, every traffic light was on green. He pulled into the car park and spotted Linda sitting in her car, he pulled in next to it. They got out.

"I'm ready for this drink," said John.

Linda was very perceptive, "Is there something you want to talk about?"

"Yes, there is," said John, but he still managed to smile. The Beeswing was busy as normal, and part of John wished it wasn't but even so, there was a table in the corner, almost as if it was waiting for John.

"I'll get the drinks, John, you sit down."

Was his ex-wife there this time? If she was, he didn't notice, he had resolved that problem and tonight he had resolved his biggest problem. He sat at the table looking out into the room observing the people, he saw Linda at the bar and then in came the silence. This was the moment of his awakening. He thought, "There is more to life than the criticisms, judgement, petty quarrels and the striving towards success, at what expense? It is at the expense of who I really am. I don't know what that is, but it is much more than what I have ever been in the past." He noticed how burdened some people were and thought to himself, "That's how I was only two weeks ago." Linda arrived with the drinks.

John had noticed her walking wasn't quite right.

"OK John, what's the problem?"

"I'll tell you in a minute, but first, have you hurt yourself? You were walking funny." Now this is the difference between being selfish and unselfish. He could have ignored the fact of Linda's physical problem and just started to discuss his own mental and emotional problems. John chose to put Linda first, and that was natural for him to do, he didn't have to think about it first and make some sort of decision as to his or Linda's needs.

"It's my right knee, I can't bend it properly and it hurts to walk on, it just came on a couple of days ago and it's getting worse."

The normal approach to this would be to consider the appropriate pain killers and recommend she goes to the hospital, there lies the first floor consciousness. That may be necessary, but what had caused Linda's knee problem?

"You haven't been kneeling in the garden too much, have you?"

"No," said Linda. It was at that moment that something started to happen to John, his hands started to get hot and that silence came in. Into his head came the thought, "Put your hands on Linda's knee, you can heal her problem." Now this is a very busy pub and it possesses a large amount of first floor consciousness, so to put his hands on Linda's knee would create an audience. John, in the past, would want to avoid that, but not now.

"Linda, do you mind if I put my hands on your knee?" John never actually said why, he could have been in trouble.

"Ok John, are you going to do hands on healing then?"

He replied, "Err yes," he said tentatively. It was obvious, thought John, that she was familiar with this, John wasn't. He placed his hands on her knee and they became even hotter. He relaxed into the silent space, not thinking anything. He even, at one point, ignored the impulse to look up to see if anyone was watching him, but nobody even noticed. They were too concerned with themselves, all but one person. It was after ten minutes that John's hands started to cool down, he assumed that was it and took them off and relaxed back into his chair, looking at Linda for a reaction. She had her eyes closed, he expected her to open them. She didn't. "What do I do? Shall I nudge her?" but something impressed him not to, so he looked briefly around the room, nobody was looking, all but one person who he did not identify with.

After about five minutes, Linda opened her eyes and smiled. "That was wonderful, the pain in gone. I didn't know you did hands on healing."

"I don't," replied John. "It just happened, but so many things have happened over the last two weeks."

Linda got up and walked around. "Yes, it's totally gone," and then sat down. "And now it's your turn," she said.

John told Linda what had happened at his mother's earlier and some of the strange things that were happening to him and that he was changing. "I don't understand it, but I like it, and I feel there is so much more to come."

Linda looked at John and was trying to choose her words, because Linda was also under-going a change, hence the right knee problem. Because knees concern moving forward in life and the ability to do that, so to an extent, Linda was slightly resisting change but on some level she knew this, but sometimes it's not easy to change things. Linda did not want to come across in any non-understandable way, she also realised her knowledge was limited.

"I think Miranda could give you some sort of a clue John, better than I could, but if you take the analogy of a house with three floors and you very much lived on the first floor, and now you are entering onto the second floor, and if we relate these three floors to conscious awareness, then you can understand the change."

"But what about the silence and stillness?" said John.

"That must be the way you access the second floor. I am guessing that as I haven't experienced it to the extent you have."

"So," said John, "there is much more to us that we realise."

"Yes," said Linda, "so much more."

John thought, "If this is an initial entrance onto the second floor, what the hell is the third floor?" John then related his experience with Helen. "I don't know what's going to happen there, at least I was true to myself even though potentially I could lose my job."

"I wouldn't worry, John. You could always set up your own business."

"Do you think so?"

"Oh yes," said Linda. There was a pause and John suddenly realised the time. He had to be home to make a phone call.

"I'm sorry, Linda, I have to go. There is a phone call I need to make." Linda smiled, almost as if she knew who he was phoning.

"Not a problem." she said and they left.

But as they were leaving, they passed a man who was standing by the door. He was tall and slim and his eyes were bright blue. John noticed him and the man made an acknowledgement with a nod, almost as if he knew John. But john didn't know him. John and Linda found themselves outside in the car park.

"Did you notice that man by the door on the way out?" asked John.

"No, I didn't think there was anyone by the door" replied Linda.

"You must have seen him, he looked like he was from a different time zone!"

"No." said Linda, "I'll see you tomorrow at work. Thanks for my healing, my knee is feeling so much better." And she gave John a peck on the cheek.

John got into his car and drove off. He had plenty of time to make it home. It started to rain quite heavily. Part of John's journey was a couple of miles in the countryside, and as he was driving down a particularly dark stretch, he noticed a car with its lights on at the side of the road and a man trying to wave him down. Part of John thought "I haven't time for this," but the other part told him to stop, and that part was starting to overtake the other part. John opened his window, the man seemed quite distressed.

He said "My car broke down and my wife is inside, she is having labour pains. I forgot to bring my mobile phone. Can I borrow yours to phone the hospital?"

"Course you can," said John grabbing for his mobile phone quickly, then he realised he hadn't charged it up. "Oh no, there's hardly any charge left."

"Worth a go," said the man. He managed to get through and then the phone went dead, just at the same time another contraction came on for his wife.

"These are getting quicker," his wife said with a tone of panic in her voice.

"There's nothing else for it," said John, "I will take you both to the hospital." John quickly cleared the back seat of his rubbish and threw it into the boot. They got in and off they sped. By this point John was as stressed as the husband was. "Two miles to go," he thought. He took a couple of gambles on the traffic lights and then overtook, guess what, a learner driver. They made the hospital just in time by the way it was going. Quickly the man thanked John and disappeared into the hospital leaving John standing there.

"Just another bizarre part of my day," thought John glancing at his watch. "Not sure whether I'll get home in time."

John walked into his kitchen at 9.55 p.m. throwing off his shoes and coat his immediate need was a beer. Into the fridge he went whipping out a bottle, holding it up in front of him "Yes, I remembered to put some in the fridge." It was reminiscent of John holding out his sock. He looked at the clock. "Was it too late to phone Miranda?" He desperately wanted to but there was something else, he needed the toilet, the drink earlier had worked its way through. What a decision, phone Miranda or go to the toilet. Unfortunately the need was greater than the desire, as he rushed to the smallest room in the house. Emerging a couple of minutes later (he could have been quicker if he had a zip instead of buttons), it was now a minute past ten. A quick glug out of the bottle, he decided to give it a go. Where was her number? He fumbled in his pockets and pulled it out, but he had slightly ripped the paper. Piecing it together he decided that the number on the tear was a seven. He dialled the number, but then quickly realised that Miranda didn't live in a residential home, he apologised and dials again changing the seven for a one, it rings, after about five rings John felt he should put the phone down. He hesitated and then it was answered.

"Hello," said Miranda.

"I am sorry," said John, "if it's too late, I'll hang up." There was a short pause, John felt a bit anguished.

"Not at all, John. I was looking forward to you phoning." Another pause. "I was quite stunned earlier when we had a hug, I haven't got over it." That broke the ice and John confirmed he felt the same. With that bit over with, as John hadn't known how to approach it, he relaxed.

"You wouldn't believe what held me up tonight," and he explained about the man at the side of the road and his wife in labour. Then he started to talk about the silence and how it was affecting his decisions. His resolution with his mother and lastly what had happened with Linda in the pub. Miranda listened, John even related some of the make-you-laugh incidents which, at the time, he hadn't but now, from a different perspective, he found highly amusing.

"My goodness John, you are certainly being impressed." John didn't quite understand that but didn't want to say so. Then he couldn't help it.

"What is that?" he said.

"Well," said Miranda, "We are not just a physical body, we possess an energy body and part of that are seven major vortexes, which are located in certain places. We can identify those places in relation to the physical body and there is one of those at the top of the head. When this particular vortex is increasing in vibration, it becomes receptive to higher frequencies that transpose themselves into impression whereby your consciousness expands into higher realms of understanding. It is also through this opening, which is known as the Crown Centre, we can, through the connection with the heart centre, transmit healing energies through the hands, just like you did with Linda."

Well, John didn't understand hardly any of that, but he needed to know, he didn't know why but there was something inside that was starting to light up. Now if he had been told that two weeks ago he would have thought, "That was a load of old rubbish," but back then John was purely intellectual and his mind was not prepared to expand itself into other concepts, it only thought from his own experience which was limited to what he saw, heard and felt.

"I have probably bombarded you with that one," said Miranda, "but you did ask." In a way Miranda was testing him out to try and give him a nudge, it worked.

"Where can I find out about all this?" said John.

"I can give you some insight, but if you seriously wish to know more about healing, you need to meet Antony, he runs courses." Miranda told John that she also did healing and worked with crystals.

"That's fascinating," said John. He was starting to become aware of his feelings for Miranda, and the same was happening to Miranda.

"Could we get together?" John nervously approached the subject, almost not wanting to ask in case she said no.

"I would love to John, but I won't be here for two weeks. I am going away." John wanted to ask her where, but something inspired him not to. "I am back for the next class at your workplace, that's the next time I will see you." Miranda's voice was creating sensations in John's heart centre, he was realising he had deep feelings for her and didn't want to wait two weeks, in fact he wished she was here now. Then he just came out with it.

"I have feelings for you, Miranda. I am going to find it hard not seeing you." There was a silence.

"I have the same feelings for you John, and I too will find it hard to wait, but this trip has come as a bit of a surprise and I need to go."

John suddenly remembered that he was only working half a day in two weeks' time. "Are you doing anything after the class?"

"No," said Miranda.

"Well, I have the afternoon off."

"That's fantastic, we'll spend some time together. Perhaps you would like to see my therapy room?"

"Great," said John.

"It's getting late," said Miranda, "and I have a long journey tomorrow."

"Ok, take care of yourself and look forward to seeing you."

"Bye, John," and she puts the phone down.

John slowly puts his phone down and standing there, he becomes lost in space. He suddenly clicks back into his mind and a big smile came over his face. "She really likes me," he thought. Suddenly a surge of belonging came over him and he relived the telephone call, he felt good about himself. But in the back of his mind he knew he had to wait two weeks, so he proceeded to finish his beer off. John wasn't feeling very sleepy, there was too much to think about so he decided on another beer. He cracked open the bottle, took a swig and moved to the back door for a smoke. He opened the door and even though it was dark, there was a light, it was the light of the moon. There was no cloud in the sky and it was a full moon. John lit his cigarette and just stared up at the moon. There was a halo of colour around it and then an unusual train of thought entered.

"You are a healer, and you will become much more than that." He was talking to himself and yet it wasn't himself, other words came. They were almost poetic and words he didn't understand. He was transfixed with this thought pattern. "Enter into your own reality, then you will know your destiny," and that was when it stopped.

"My goodness, there's a lot going on," and John suddenly started to feel tired. He finished his beer and decided to go to bed. Lying in bed the whole day seemed to run through his head and when he finally caught up with himself, he fell asleep.

Two Weeks Later:

The alarm clock shrills its message into the space, the room resounds to its repetitive sound, growing louder by the second, a hand reaches out and switches the alarm off. He lay there thinking, "It's that day again".

"Well," he thought "I have sorted out the clothes problem, the food problem and the mother problem." He felt a sense of freedom. Also he was going to see Miranda today. There was one thing that lay at the back of his mind, and that was Helen. It had been two weeks since the presentation and no word. In fact, he hadn't even seen her so he had just carried on doing what he was doing, bypassing the paperwork.

John leapt out of bed. He had prepared everything, clean socks, an ironed shirt, but he had forgotten to buy some razor blades. This was the third day, so his face was looking a little rough. Now these days it is an in thing to do, but his company being fairly traditional, required a good turnout. It was never said, but it didn't need to be, as the managing director was an icon of smart perfection. Also John had neglected his hair cut, it wasn't that long, but with the stubble he certainly wasn't that pristine. John hadn't quite realised because he hadn't seriously looked at himself in the mirror. He was getting too busy to take any notice. But something also in the back of his mind told him the managing director was due for a visit. "I need a shave," he thought and moved swiftly into the bathroom and then it dawned. "Oh shit! I never bought any razor blades." He approached the mirror, almost not wanting to look in it, but he had no choice. Now when he first looked it was very superficially, trying to view himself as a whole and not really focussing. "Not too bad," he thought," and then he zoomed in a little but more. He started to view his stubble. He turned his head to the right and then the left. That was fatal because front on looked better. Even moving back from the mirror he still looked rough. John had quite a big bathroom and at about six feet he didn't look bad, of course the clock was ticking away, but a saving grace he was now setting his clock 25 minutes earlier. "Where is my razor?," he found it instantly, it still had a blade in it, but the last time he used it, it pulled and he ended up with a sore face, and of course he now had three days growth - a disaster if you use a blunt razor.

"Maybe it wouldn't be that bad if I used more foam." It was a picture, John looking in the mirror holding his razor up close to his face trying to make a decision. "It wouldn't work," he thought, "I must go to the shop later." But will

John have time to do that? He brushed his hair. "Blimey, it's longer than I thought."

Anyway, he cleans his teeth, dresses and heads downstairs, still with plenty of time even for a cup of tea. John had a bounce in his step, he was thinking about lunch time. He packs his lunch and heads for the door. He unlocks it and was just about to open it when the phone rings. I think John has been here before and this time he hesitates. He could become aloof and walk out, this obviously would be a natural opposite reaction to how he used to be. But many people choose not to answer the phone for many reasons, it is simply a case of avoiding certain people in their life, 'If you cannot handle it, don't answer it' - is their philosophy. This is not discrimination but avoidance, unresolved issues. One could ask what's the difference?

Well, discrimination takes into account cause and effect, whereas avoidance just decides not to interact now. In a way John's haste answering the phone to his mother, set about a chain of events whereby there was no choice but to resolve his issues, not because John had contacted the second floor consciousness. But then in a way, that consciousness brought about the chance to form a better relationship with his mother through an understanding of her. Relationships are what life is all about, "right relationships." John was starting to form right relationships and that was because they were starting to be based upon truth, and that in relationship to himself and then others. So will John answer the phone? Now John's phone gives the number that is calling, he had organised that a week ago. It started to sound familiar. John answered the phone.

"Hello John, it's Miranda. I'm back and thought I'd catch you to say I am looking forward to seeing you. I couldn't stop myself, I had to ring you."

"I'm glad you did, I've been thinking about you a lot and wondered how you were."

"I'm OK, hopefully that trip will sort things out. Anyway, would you give me a hug when I see you?"

"I'll give you more than one! Sorry about that!"

"That's OK John. I'll see you later."

"Bye Miranda," and John put the phone down.

When lots of issues are resolved, phone calls then tend to be a positive interaction, unless of course people are trying to sell you something and that is an area where discrimination comes in.

John felt good, he was so pleased she had phoned and out the door he went. Now one issue he hadn't resolved was the fact that next door's dog had a habit of pooing on John's drive. Now with John's feel good factor, he would have had a disaster, it was almost as if the dog did it on purpose trying to catch John out. The dog had been let out half an hour earlier into the back garden, but this dog was crafty, it could jump the joining fence and then, once it has done the business, jumped back again. The owner was starting to worry that the dog was constipated.

John approached his car, it would only take one more step, and measuring the distance of his steps, you could see where his foot would land. (I could be quite graphic at this point but I will leave this to your imagination). Something told him to look down, as his foot was on the way down and approximately six inches away, perhaps it was the smell that caught his attention as it was still steaming. John miraculously did a hop scotch movement, he then stood staring down. Now the old John would have then gone into obscenities which we won't mention, but this was the new John standing there. "I think I need to sort this out," he thought.

Now John didn't know that the owner never let the dog out in the front, so he could easily assume that the owner was irresponsible, and it is not good to assume anything, it could lead to wrong action. We could extend this concept to what we hear, read or see. It is well to discriminate these things, are they in line with truth? And people and newspapers, to quote instances, have a habit of glamorising events to such an extent that the truth gets lost. Yes, some people's lives are so dull they have to do this to evoke a reaction.

John looked at his watch, is there time for this? But his desire to stop this happening was so great he decided there was and walked over, pausing briefly at the front door.

"Let's get this over with," he thought. He made a firm knock at the door and waited for a response, he hadn't actually thought about what he was going to say, which might have been a good idea. His next door neighbour appeared at the door, she was stressed. Her credit card was missing and generally things financially weren't very good, in fact they were horrible. She was trying to consolidate her loans but wasn't good at that sort of thing. Her husband used to do all that, but he had left a year ago, consequently she was a bit of a mess, and John could see that in her face.

"Hello John," she said. John looked at her realising her condition.

"Hello, Janet. I just wondered how you were because I hadn't seen you in the garden or anything."

"I'm not good John, I'm just so stressed."

"Can I help?" said John.

"Maybe," said Janet, but she was a very proud person and didn't like to ask for help. All thoughts of the dog had disappeared from John's mind. It wasn't appropriate to mention that. Janet's condition was far worse than John stepping in some dog poo. This situation is worth thinking about and applying to life.

Janet was hesitating, John stepped in.

"I am very good at financial things." He had unconsciously picked up on Janet's problems.

"Are you?" she said.

"Yes."

"Then maybe you can help. You are an angel, but you have to go to work. Can I speak to you later?"

Now John was very busy later and he was honest about that. "I will try and get you during my break at work and then speak to you properly tomorrow night. Is that OK?"

"Of course, John. I feel so relieved someone can help me. I have been asking for help."

"What did she mean, asking for help? Who from?" he thought. "I'll speak to you later, Janet."

"Thanks, John."

John turned to walk away and he couldn't help but notice in her window was a picture of an angel with some crystals surrounding it.

He got into his car, obviously avoiding what was previously mentioned, and gently pulled off the drive. "Perhaps Janet was asking for help from that angel picture," and he started to think about that. Could help come from somewhere other than what we can see or perceive? John was starting to think very deep thoughts. Is there more than just this life? Are there other dimensions and are they connected in some way?

That was very deep John, but it is worthwhile thinking about these things. Is there some sort of force and energy that creates things to happen according to how we think or feel?

As he was driving to work what immediately come into his mind was the learner driver. It seems that every two weeks things occur, and he thought about the two incidents with the learner driver, both ending up with some sort of disaster on John's part. He instantly deduced in both cases, it was to do with smoking a cigarette, quick as a flash he thought, "I'll have the cigarette when I get to work," therefore any mishap cannot occur.

It actually doesn't work that way, but if John is feeling secure with that, maybe we won't mention that if the same frustration is there, then it will manifest slightly differently, but nonetheless it will manifest. Because John is in a process of awakening these things have a habit of coming up fast.

Even though John felt secure, there was still an underlying unease and he found himself looking at every turn to see if he could see the learner driver. What a massive coincidence it would be if it turned up for the third time, and sure enough, it did.

John was on a clear road. "No learner driver in sight," he thought. He pulled up at the traffic lights. "It's not going to happen this time." He happened to glance in his mirror and there behind him was the learner driver, but not just any old learner driver, the same learner driver as the previous weeks.

"I cannot believe it, it's here again, but this time it's behind me. Does this mean I have now left this experience behind?" Maybe John.

John was nonetheless getting slightly nervous, as an automatic response he went for his cigarettes, then instantly thought better of it. He pulled away from the lights, "Anyway," he thought, "if it's behind me then nothing can happen." He stopped at the next set of lights, they turned to green and anxious to pull away, John stalled his car. This wasn't a good time for this to happen, and he started to mess up not knowing whether he was in gear or not. He kangarooed forward. Looking in the mirror, he could see their faces. Now they weren't saying anything, but the instructor's face told the story as he scowled at the back of John's head, the learner driver was slightly panicking, not knowing what was happening. John quickly retrieved his poise, started the engine and pulled away just as the lights were changing, consequently the learner driver was left sitting at the lights.

"Oh well, that's sorted that out," as John carried on, arriving at work with ten minutes to spare. He jumped out of his car and moved around the side of the building to have a quick puff.

He lit his cigarette and started to think about his day when a side door suddenly opened, out stepped Helen. "Nobody uses that door," thought John. He suddenly felt uncomfortable as he had always concealed the fact that he smoked. Something impressed him not to quickly throw it away. "You don't have to justify yourself," came into his head.

"Hello, John, I didn't know you smoked," was the comment as she approached him.

"What a pain in the neck she is," he thought. What was going to be his comment? Will he enter into a dialogue about the fact that he smoked, then try to justify this, and try to portray the fact that he is seeking to quit? John didn't.

"Good morning Helen, it's a beautiful day." He totally diverted the situation.

"Didn't you know that's bad for you?"

"You're bloody bad for me," thought John. Again he didn't answer but informed Helen he was only working half a day.

"I was going to have a meeting with you this afternoon. I have been away for two weeks and have been thinking about your presentation and your action regarding this."

It suddenly dawned on John why she hadn't come back to him. He was brought to a silence and didn't respond, hoping that Helen would break the silence as to whether she would insist on a meeting or delay it for another day. She did.

"Is it possible to alter your plans John?"

"No, I have something important to do." Helen is not used to being turned down, well not professionally. She looked at John seriously then turned and walked away. Watching her disappear through the door John took one last puff.

"That didn't go down too well," he thought. "Best get to work." John walked into the office, the only thing he could sense was his own feelings concerning the encounter with Helen. "I need a coffee," he thought, and there at the coffee machine was Jane, just like two weeks previous.

"How are you John?" said Jane. "I saw Helen talking to you outside the building. Was she talking to you about the managing director's visit today?"

"Err, no," said John. "What time is he coming?"

"Not sure, it could be before or after lunch. I've heard he's not very happy."

"Oh no," thought John, "he's not going to like my appearance. That's funny Helen wanting a meeting this afternoon." John was not sure about all this. He fumbled in his pocket for some change for the coffee machine, just as Trevor turned up.

"Hello Trevor. Have you any change?"

"I have loads of it. It's a good job I have a belt on, otherwise my trousers might fall down!" smiling he took out his change. "I'll buy you a coffee." Trevor was distinctly a different person from two weeks ago.

"How do you like it John?"

"Black, two sugars, please." The machine whined away, down came a cup and it started to fill up.

"I've heard a few whispers John, about your delivery strategy. I think it's a great idea, but I daren't attempt it because I think Helen's got it in for you."

"What do you mean?" said John.

"Well, said Trevor as he put in the money for another coffee, down came the cup. "I think she…. Oh no! I forgot to take the other coffee out!" There is a bit of déjà vu with this, only it's a reverse situation. John started laughing, the boot was on the other foot. Trevor also saw the funny side of it, but did Helen, who was walking towards them? John hadn't noticed.

"What were you going to tell me about Helen?" John asked.

"Not now John, she's walking towards us."

"I hope someone is going to clear this up." She threw John a look of disapproval and then walked off.

"I will sort it out Trevor, I'm used to this sort of thing," said John, wondering what Helen's problem with him was.

"Thanks John," and off went Trevor with John none the wiser. John cleared things up and went to his desk, he started to think about things. "I haven't been happy here for a long time," he thought, "but I haven't had the confidence to do anything about it, it's almost as if they were doing me a favour giving me a job." He then looked around. "This place stifles me, perhaps I need to seriously think about moving on."

The phone rang, it was a customer he rarely spoke to, they basically only used John to top up their own supplies, in short they are suppliers as well, almost competitors, it depends how you define that word. It was a guy called Adam.

"I have recently become manager and I am looking to project this company into the future in exciting new ways, so speed and flow are important to us. I need an order, when can we expect it?"

"When do you want it?" asked John.

"Today." Now this was taking things into another dimension.

"There will be a small cost but I can offset this with some discount. Your delivery will be with you by 4 p.m."

"Make it 3 p.m. and we have a deal," replied Adam.

"OK, thank you for your order."

This really is now challenging any red tape that exists within John's company. It is also challenging John to find the solution. Into his head came the thought, "Organise this, as if this was your company." That is an interesting concept, "as if," which assumes that is, what it is, and yet it has the ability to change the present, not necessarily to exactly what you are treating "as if", but it has a dynamic energetic effect upon the future.

John is now purposely attempting to create his future. He is breaking down the barriers and out of the confines that existed externally, and using the assumption that something can happen, then there is a possibility for its manifestation and appearance. Impossibilities, so called, only exist within our intellectual and emotional ways of thinking and feeling. Can we create our future by simply thinking about it? Through thought, we can create the substance necessary for it to continue its journey from being a thought, into a physical manifestation of that thought. Energy follows thought, especially if it has intention and specifically a vision. John's vision as yet is not clear, he would not be able to answer the question "have you a vision?" and obviously a vision concerns the future, potential future.

John's state of consciousness and circumstances at the start of this very short journey, from where we picked up on his life when the alarm bell first rang on that first morning, was not capable of creating a vision and certainly not manifesting it, but many things have happened since, so he is now clearing the path and when the sun shines upon his clear path, his vision will appear.

Well, according to the clock John has five hours to organise and deliver the order as it is now 10 a.m. Another snag, is he has two and a half hours to do it in as he is off this afternoon, and this is not just any afternoon. Also it will take two hours to get to the customer, no pressure at all really. His initial thoughts weren't focussed, he needed to clear the mists from his mind, then he started to formulate his approach. First thing, organise the transport. That was a bit tricky but they agreed, they could sense John's passion for his work. "Well, I've organised the last bit," he thought, "now for the rest. If I shove this order to the top of the list, we can make it." There was only one problem, to meet the other deadlines someone would have to work overtime. The company adopted a policy of no overtime unless they were completely in the shit, and then they would if they could give time off in lieu. Yes, this company watched every penny, they didn't understand the word 'flexibility' as a creative power, or how money is a substance that needs to flow. They need to understand the concept of money.

John phoned the Stores, their response was a little icy - talk about negative. John had to think quickly as there was a distinct 'power in the job' situation and they were not prepared to bend the rules.

"It will only take an extra hour to do this," said John. "It's worth a case of beer." Now here we see the difference between goods and money, goods take away the element of choice that money has, but if the goods are chosen wisely, and John knew that the stores staff loved a beer, then he could be on a winner. He was.

"OK, make that two and I'll do it."

This was going to cost John money, not the company's money, but then he was assuming the "as if" it was his company. "All sorted," thought John. He felt pleased with himself and why shouldn't he? Some things need to be acknowledged. It was approaching lunchtime and John was looking forward to seeing Miranda again, but first he started to ponder his situation with the company.

"I am probably starting to push this a little too far," he thought, "Perhaps I need to move on." Now this would have been inconceivable, he wasn't one to take chances, in fact John was now a totally different person in just a short time, but then something was pushing John further up the house.

He was now putting the second floor consciousness into action and in so doing, a small light was starting to filter down from the third floor. He was rapidly overcoming his first floor tendencies, through lifting his mind onto the second floor, he also was realising this. John was becoming accustomed to gaining insight through the silence, and he was starting to realise how to obtain this silence. Then suddenly an idea came to him, "I wonder if the company who just placed the order was looking to employ new people." He remembered a new person was in charge who is quite dynamic. "Perhaps I should give him a ring," and then the thought came to him, "Perhaps after the order has been delivered, I think I need to phone them this afternoon to confirm this."

Linda suddenly walked past. "Are we on again tonight John? By the way, the knee's still a lot better. Could you give it another go? I think that will do it. Are you looking forward to the class at lunchtime John?" as she sat down next to him. She smiled.

"I think she knows something I don't," thought John. "Yes, I am," he replied and the moment he responded to Linda his hands suddenly started to get hot, just like in the pub. But then Linda had sat close to him, so therefore their electromagnetic fields were interacting and because of Linda's problem, John's vibrations were responding.

John quickly looked at the time. "Hmm 15 minutes to lunchtime, do you fancy a quick go now?"

"Are you offering me a quickie, John?"

John smiled, replying "I'm not good with an audience. My hands are getting hot, shall I try to heal your knee now?"

"OK," said Linda, "I'll take up your offer."

John put his hand on Linda's knee. It was more intense this time and the silence he felt was incredible. John would say it felt timeless. After a few minutes John really got into the space and was totally zoned in, but he started to perceive a whisper coming from Linda.

She was saying, "We are being watched, John." He carried on.

"Who by?" asked John.

"Helen and the managing director."

"Are they close?" said John.

"Not really, they are by Helen's office." The heat was still pouring through John's hands. He wondered whether he should stop, and as an automatic reaction he tried to lift his hands away, but he couldn't, they were stuck to Linda's knee like a magnet. "Great," he thought. "Best start looking for another job." And he continued.

"What are they doing now, Linda?"

"They are talking to each other. Oh, they are starting to go back into Helen's office." It was at that point the heat in John's hands started to subside and the healing was finished.

Linda stood up. "That's great John, thanks. Time for the class, let's go."

"I'll be with you in a minute Linda." She walked away and John slumped over his desk.

Retrieving his sense of space and time, he stood up and made his way to the class where Miranda was waiting with a smile. There was a brief hug and John quickly squeezed her hand as he walked into the room. He sat down and waited in silence for the class to start. There was a slight seriousness about John, he was accepting the fact that things were changing. In short, a transformation was happening within himself, which was being reflected in the outside world, and in that case, his job and relationships.

He can see the connection between the inner and outer worlds, maybe all those earlier challenges will not repeat themselves. If we take two instances: the first with the learner driver, it doesn't mean John will never be held up by a learner driver, but his attitude towards it will have changed, therefore it will present no problems and, of course, any resultant cause and effect, and it was quite obvious what the effects were. The second, well not wishing to be crude, concerns the dog poo and his shoes, and of course we all end up in that sometimes, but the chances of John doing that again have greatly diminished.

As he sat waiting, John was experiencing the silence, his mind was clear and he felt calm. In fact his mind was more than calm, it was actively present, and then the second floor consciousness really started to impress him. He felt love, he felt compassion, he started to receiving insight into healing, and, he was thinking many things that he had never thought about before.

Miranda sat down in front of the group, virtually opposite John, who was starting to radiate energy. She picked that up and told the group just to shut their eyes and spend a few minutes relaxing. Through John's second floor connection, he was radiating energy through his electromagnetic field into the room, and guess what that energy was? It was healing energy.

Miranda felt this energy and instructed the group to imagine a pathway of golden light, it took them into a beautiful garden where they could experience all the colour and scents. She introduced them also to the security that the tree represents, she knew that this would aid John. The healing was affecting the area of her body where she had a problem. Heat was emanating from John's hands and they started to lift up. He was already aware of what was happening and chose to go with it. Part of him was thinking "What the hell is going on?" but the other part of him felt comfortable with this fact, because let us not forget, 'John has something to do in this life' and this something is his destiny. This went on for fifteen minutes until suddenly John relaxed his attention and opened his eyes. He looked around and waited, everyone was still sitting with their eyes closed, even Miranda. Expecting them to open their eyes quickly, John was surprised when they didn't, in fact it was a good five minutes before this started to happen. Gradually everyone became fully conscious in the room and started to chat about the experience. John felt a little embarrassed and almost wanted to leave quickly, then Miranda spoke.

"That was remarkable John," and then several people started to say that their physical problems had disappeared, others said that they lost track of time and some experienced colour flashing through their inner screen.

"What was happening?" thought John. "How can I affect people at a distance?" and then it dawned on him - what is the difference between 12 feet and 12 miles, would it take longer to reach 12 miles? And the answer to that John, is "No," because what you see as the space between objects, is the same space as 12 miles away. What you do in one portion of space can happen also in another portion of space, the distance is irrelevant. John hadn't quite come to that conclusion but he will, including many other things.

Miranda picked up on the theme of colours and how each colour possesses a certain vibration, and how what we wear can relate to our particular mood and psychology. She also touched briefly upon the higher streams of energy consciousness and their relevant colours. The class then came to an end and they filtered themselves back to work, leaving just John and Miranda.

"I've missed you," said John as he held her hand.

"I have you, John. That was remarkable what you have just done."

"I don't know what's going on, but I seem to be able to heal with my hands."

"Yes, you can. Some people call it a gift but I believe it is something we all possess, it just takes something in life to trigger it into action. It's almost like a different state of consciousness and one aspect of this is compassion, but sometimes someone is destined to be a healer and I think you are, John."

"What do I do now then?" said John.

"Put it to the test and start to use it," said Miranda.

"I am not sure about that." John was having doubts.

"Look," said Miranda, "the most wonderful thing in the world is to be able to heal someone from their pain, and pain is not just physical, it can be emotional or mental or all three. Look what you have done today."

John thought about it and also remembered Linda's knee. "You're right," he said. "Anyway, what shall we do this afternoon?"

"Well, you could give me a hug to start with - best move away from the door though." So they did, all thought disappeared from John as they embraced each other. After a while of intense feeling, Miranda broke away.

"Why don't you come to my place, I'll show you my healing and meditation room?"

We pause and consider, if this was John's first floor consciousness - he would think he was on a winner, but it isn't. He has no such designs because for any relationship to work, it has to be on all levels, on all three floors ultimately, but for the sake of understanding, the physical, emotional and mental levels but also spiritual levels. Therefore each one has to be in balance with each other. Many relationships fail because of an over-emphasis on the physical. A whole book could be written upon the subject from the second floor consciousness.

"I would love to," John replied, "Where do you live?" Miranda gave John the address.

"I'll see you there then," she turned, smiled at John and walked away.

"I just have a few things I need from my desk," thought John. He stopped at the doorway, he could see Helen and the managing director walking around the office floor. It looked like they were heading for Linda. "Perhaps I won't," he thought and he did a quick left, heading for the exit. Unfortunately John kicked a rubbish bin, it's a good job it wasn't a bucket! It must have drawn attention. Quick as a flash John was out of the door, jumped into his car and off he went. "I'll worry about all that tomorrow. Now, where am I going?" He found the piece of paper with the address on. "OK, here we go then," John was feeling somewhat liberated.

If we consider that John might well be in trouble, why was he feeling liberated? Well, he had released himself from the constraints he had put upon himself, also those that held him within the first floor consciousness in the outer world. The second floor consciousness sees no restrictions, just experiences that lead one out of Karma and onto the path of destiny.

John found the address and pulled onto the drive. It was quite a beautiful semi-detached Georgian house. Miranda was waiting at the door.

"Come in John." Slightly nervous, John entered. He was always worried about the way he came across, so he normally tried to behave perfectly according to what he believed that to be. This was starting to fall away, but there was still some patterning.

"Would you like a drink, John?"

"A coffee would be nice, thanks," replied John.

"This way then," and into the kitchen they went. Miranda made the drinks and they then sat down at the table. "I have to go away tomorrow for another couple of weeks, John."

His heart sank slightly, he had already missed her, although as yet they hadn't formed a relationship. A normal reaction is to ask 'where are you going?', but John was inclined to let Miranda take the lead. He also detected a note that something wasn't quite right. There was a pause. John waited.

"I first got into all this stuff some years ago when I became ill. I was slightly interested before, but never pursued it. I was always too busy with my job, pleasing other people and being careful with money and I think all that contributed to my illness, and that certainly was a wake-up call. So, I changed my life and attitude and became well again, my husband didn't like the changes, so we parted. You are the first man I have felt anything for since, and we've only known each other a few weeks, and briefly at that."

"I know," said John. "I feel the same way about you." He held her hands, it came into his mind that the illness some years ago had come back, but he didn't say anything. He didn't need to as Miranda also knew that John had picked something up. He looked at Miranda and he then felt a pressure of energy on his forehead and started to perceive in his mind images of her electromagnetic field, imagining dark patches among a sea of swirling colour. John closed his eyes and imagined a light above his head and that light surrounded his head into his forehead, in fact it intensified at a point between his eyebrows. He opened his eyes, still with the image of the dark patches, a beam of light shot out from the point between the eyebrows and started to dissipate one of the dark patches.

"Are you healing?" said Miranda.

John was so focussed he could only say "I am getting rid of dark patches that are surrounding you."

"I can feel something happening John."

John removed the dark patches and then released the tension of the experience and slumped down onto the kitchen table. He was quite used to doing that in the office but for different reasons, he was trying to assimilate the experience. But then there was a unique stillness present and John's hands started to heat up.

"Where is the problem Miranda? I need to use the hands."

"It's down here John, but I need to lie down."

"OK, where?"

"Follow me," and she led him into her healing meditation room where she got onto the couch.

John was in the zone and took no notice of the room, he went straight into hands on. The heat increased, but this time there was also a vibration present and certain words were coming into John's head, all of a healing nature. One can only surmise they were connected to alleviating the problem and possibly the cause of the problem. The healing lasted just over 15 minutes and as John lifted his hands away, he noticed Miranda had fallen asleep. Was she asleep as we know it or was it a healing sleep, which still retains an amount of consciousness with the surroundings?

John was inspired to quietly leave the room. He went to the back door and lit up a smoke, he started to ponder deeply about the healing, and the words came into his head, "you can heal this problem." He put his cigarette out, washed his hands and went back to the healing room. He pushed the door open and it looked like the room was full of light. It was a sunny day but this looked more than this.

"Are you alright Miranda?" said John in a soft voice.

She opened her eyes. "Yes, I am. I felt something change inside me."

Once more John felt the need not to ask anything.

Miranda got off the couch and into a chair, John sat opposite her. The room had a stillness. Next to him were some crystals, John picked one up and placed it between Miranda's feet and he gave her one to hold.

"I'm sorry, I just felt inspired to do that, I didn't know why," he said.

"Thank you John, I'm feeling grounded now."

To John being 'grounded' was a childhood thing when he wasn't allowed out, which happened quite often. He felt his mind running with this. Miranda interrupted his train of thought, which is just as well.

"I'll explain what grounding is next time we meet."

"In two weeks' time?" asked John.

"Yes."

He was feeling sad about that.

Miranda held his hand. "It's alright John, after that we can see each other more regularly."

John looked at Miranda and then he just came out with it, "Would you mind if I gave you a kiss?"

This definitely confirmed how they felt about each other, it was soft and loving with a certain amount of passion, and that is as far as it went.

They moved back into the kitchen, the time had flown.

"I have things to do before I leave tomorrow John."

"OK," said John as they moved towards the front door. "I'm meeting Linda at the Beeswing in a while."

"I've heard you healed her knee."

"Well, hopefully. I could give it another go, but in the pub it is a little noticeable, although I don't think anybody noticed.

All but a man standing in the corner by the door, it was almost as if he had observed me to see how I was doing."

"Maybe he was John. You can never tell a book by its cover. Was he wearing strange clothes?"

"Yes, how did you know that?"

"Oh, I just guessed."

It was time to leave and they kissed once more before John left. He was feeling so happy and yet a slight sadness. "This is going to be a long two weeks" he thought as he drove off. He was going to meet Linda. There was no problem with learner drivers and in no time he pulled into the car park.

Linda wasn't there, he checked his watch, he was a few minutes late. "I wonder where she is?" He decided to wait, and wait. He looked at the time, she was now 15 minutes late. "That's odd," then just as John was thinking to ring her, she appeared in the car park.

John approached Linda, "Is everything alright?"

"No John, I've had to go to mum's as she has a terrible back pain. The pain killers have helped but she is in a lot of trouble. Anyway, shall we go in?"

John thought about this, "No," he said, "I can help your mother if you take me over there, we can have a drink after."

"Are you sure, John? You are so kind," and off they went in Linda's car. It wasn't very far and they parked up.

"I'll go and say why you are here first, if that's all right."

"Of course."

After a few minutes Linda came out and said, "Anything you can do she would be grateful for."

"OK," said John and in he went. Linda's mum was sitting on the sofa. "Where does it hurt?" asked John.

"It's my lower back."

"I need to put my hands on where it hurts, could you lie down?" Linda's mum made herself comfortable, although her lower back was hurting. John brought himself to a stillness and then placed his hands on her back. They were becoming hot, he also felt the tension within her body. It took a while before a complete resonance could occur, then he felt her body start to relax. He continued until the heat started to subside, then he asked "How does it feel now?"

"The pain has gone." John gently lifted his hands away and Sylvia gradually sat up, stood up, stretched and then sat down again.

"That's wonderful," she said. "That was draining me and the pain killers hardly touched it."

"I am glad I could help," said John.

"Are you all right now mum?" said Linda.

"Yes, my dear," she replied.

"OK, I'll see you tomorrow," and John and Linda then left.

Driving back to the pub Linda told John how grateful she was for his help. They pulled into the car park.

"I could do with a beer," John remarked.

"You deserve one," replied Linda and in they went.

It wasn't quite so busy tonight, so they were served quickly and they sat down.

"It's been another one of those days," said John. He started to relax, then for whatever reason glanced over his shoulder towards the door, and there was the same man standing in the corner.

"Linda," he said, "can you see that man over there?" Just as he said that, a crowd of people came into the pub, so Linda did not see the man.

"No John. Are you worried about this person?"

"No, but I feel he is watching me, though not in a disturbing way."

"Perhaps he's your overshadowing spiritual soul," laughed Linda.

"I hope not," replied John. "He might not approve of me being in a pub, let alone drinking."

"I don't think that would bother him, it's what you can do for other people that counts and you have certainly done that today."

"I know," said John, "I find it quite unbelievable and feel I need to write down what has occurred, particularly how it happened, and also I feel there is so much more."

How true is that, John, there is so much more and to realise that opens the door to the second floor consciousness.

"Well," said John, "perhaps we can have an uneventful drink."

"That would be boring John. What can you conjure up tonight," said Linda smiling. Well, as soon as she said that, John felt the need to turn around again and look behind him. "How interesting," he thought. "It's Helen, what's she doing here?" He is referring to the officer manager and then suddenly he realised, "Oh no, talk about tracking one down. Can you see who's just come into the pub Linda?"

"Yes I can. She's actually with someone and it's not her husband!"

"Really," said John and he was now finding it hard not to laugh.

"She appears to be all over him John. Oh dear, he's just fondled her bottom and she's smiling."

"Well this is a turn up for the book, perhaps she might extend that smile into the office, but then, could I keep a straight face?" John thought about it. "She's obviously not happy, Linda. Perhaps I should look at it that way."

"Good idea. John, are you going to actively pursue healing?"

"Possibly," replied John. "I am going to give it some thought. I know nothing about it, but I know I can help people."

"I would, you could practice on Miranda." Again, John felt it wise not to ask why. Then Linda came out with it, "Are you two getting together?" she asked with a smile.

John was thrown briefly - you have been working with truth John, what are you going to say? "It's looking that way," he replied.

"Oh good, I am so pleased for you both." Linda looked at her watch. "I need to go, can we meet again in two weeks?"

"I would love to Linda," and they started to leave the Beeswing.

John thought it wise not to try to see where Helen was, but he couldn't help sling a glance over his left shoulder. I don't think Helen would have noticed John even if he was standing in front of her, she was too busy. They made their way to the door, Linda went first, and there was the man standing in the corner. As John passed him, he nodded and smiled with a look of knowing. His eyes were bright blue, there was certainly something different about him.

John and Linda reached the car park.

"What do you think about the man standing in the corner Linda?"

"What man? There was nobody there."

John didn't know what to say. He could have insisted the man was there, but thought better of it and decided to take the experience home with him.

"Goodbye John," and Linda gave him a hug "see you tomorrow."

"Goodnight Linda," and they both drove out of the car park.

John headed home. A lot had happened today. "It's not an unusual occurrence," he thought. "It seems to run every two weeks, coincidentally with Miranda's class at work." He drove home without incident, pulled up onto the drive and then realised he had promised to help Janet next door. He had intended to go straight to her door, which he started to do, then suddenly he realised he needed the loo, and no better than the one you've been used to. There is some sort of security within your own personal four walls, unless of course a lot of people live in the house, then your own space becomes everyone else's and the loo becomes an escape. Into his house he flashed, nobody else lived there, so no need to shut the door as long as you have shut the front door. A flushing noise was heard and John left the loo slightly slower than when he had entered. As he walked down the corridor he noticed his answer phone flashing. He was in a hurry to sort out Janet, with her finances, but could that be a message from Miranda? He pressed the play button and was slightly disappointed that it wasn't, but when he started to hear the message, that feeling disappeared. It was Trevor asking for help and the surprising thing was, he wanted John's help with his healing. Trevor was in the class today and experienced the healing for himself, but it was not for himself that he was requesting. It was quite a long message that touched his heart. Trevor was not at work tomorrow and ended his call asking John to ring him in the morning if he could.

"I'll listen to that later," thought John and headed next door. He rang the bell and Janet opened the door.

"Thank you for coming John, I thought you would forget about me, just like everyone else."

"Janet is certainly at crisis point," thought John. She led him into the dining room and on the table was a stack of papers. They sat down.

"Let's work through your income and expenditure," said John, starting to get to work on it. After a while he felt some sort of presence. No, it wasn't the silence, it was Janet's dog which headed towards John, almost with a smile on its face. Now, John's experience of this dog has all been to do with one thing, which is probably a common factor with his position at work. To John's horror the dog sat on his foot, John had politely taken his shoes off on entering the house, (he obviously was now fully on top of his sock problem). John froze. What was it going to do? Is this the dog's chance to finally crap on John? He looked at Janet, who never said a word. She didn't know what to say. I think she was embarrassed, especially as the dog had just farted on John's foot! She knew this as the smell was reaching her nostrils and now it was reaching John's.

He didn't know what to do or say and then Janet started to laugh. "I'm sorry John, you've come to help me and my dog has farted on your foot," and she howled with uncontrollable laughter.

"Oh well," thought John, "at least that has cheered her up." Yes it had. The pendulum had swung. Janet hadn't laughed for a long time, that's possibly why she couldn't control it now, although it *was* funny.

She managed to say, "Get off John's foot and out you go Gabe," and the dog left the room.

"I need to stand up a minute Janet"

"Fine. Will you excuse me a moment?" Well Janet had laughed so much she was in danger of wetting herself and she left the room.

Everything calmed down and John worked out a plan for Janet. "It's not as bad as you think Janet," and he explained.

"Thank you John," they moved towards the front door. "I do apologise for earlier."

"Well, it's cheered you up," smiled John. "I think whenever I get depressed, if I think about it, I will cheer up. By the way," said John, "that's an unusual name for a dog."

"Oh, it's short for Gabriel," and she pointed to a picture of an angel.

"That's nice," replied John, thinking he'd just been farted on by a dog named after an archangel! John left.

"Thanks again," called Janet.

John acknowledged with a wave and opened his front door. Guess where he went? No, that was second as he needed the security room first. Then straight to the fridge, he had a choice between a not so strong or a strong beer. The strong one won. Off went the bottle top as he entered into a moment of sheer bliss, this was his favourite beer. Moment over, he went back to the message on his answer phone to digest what Trevor was saying. He had to skip a few first, and then Trevor's voice came over. He could tell there was a hint of distress by his tone. Trevor was asking John if he could do some healing on someone he knew. There wasn't anything that was working so John was a bit of a last resort, sometimes it's like that. Trevor finished with "Please John, could you help?"

John put the phone down. "I have to help," he thought. He also realised he needed to write down his experiences of healing from earlier. "Maybe that will also give me a clue as to what to do." He grabbed a notebook which he had been bought at Christmas, incidentally by his Mother, it had a beautiful cover. At the time John thought "Why do I need this?" but sometimes things are set in motion well before they start to happen. He sat down with his pen, "Now, what happened?" he thought.

He was struggling to remember, then he thought maybe the silence would help, and it did. John started to write, but also other things were coming into his head and he wrote them down. A good hour passed without a pause until John wrote the last word. "I'll re-read that tomorrow, it's getting late."

Then his mind went to Miranda.

He was momentarily tired, but that was fast passing as he was reliving the kiss they had earlier, and then the fact dawned upon him that he would have no contact for two weeks. A wave of emptiness came over him, he felt a bit lost and started to walk around the house, not concentrating on anything but the occasional slurp of beer.

Then he heard a knock at the door. "Who is that, it's quite late?" He opened the door and couldn't believe his eyes. It was Miranda! He was speechless.

"Hello John. If it's all right with you, I would like to stay the night, but if you are too busy, then I don't mind, I will just go home."

"No, please stay," said John. "Come in."

"I thought I would bring you something. I have two bottles of beer for you." and she walked into the house.

As John was pushing the door to, he noticed a ray of light and looked up. There was a thin slither of moon in the night sky, a new moon. John smiled and he closed the door.

THE END

Part Two – Johns Challenge

About the Author

Andrew Carter's life is dedicated to his work. His Destiny is to bring illumination to peoples minds and to alleviate as much pain and suffering as possible. This he does through his healing, teaching and writing, helping to raise consciousness so there is more compassion and integration with the methods of dealing with disease and the approach to health.

He has been healing since 1996 and runs crystal and healing courses at The Rose School in Northamptonshire.

Forthcoming Books of the Series:

John's Challenge

The Word

The Last Word

Dark Night of the Soul

The Reunion

A Strange Encounter

COVID 19

Full Circle

Andrew can be contacted via his websites:

www.crystaltherapycourses.com

Or www.thecrystalbarn.co.uk

www.ingramcontent.com/pod-product-compliance
Lightning Source LLC
LaVergne TN
LVHW061036070526
838201LV00073B/5065